S0-APN-009

STRAND

$2 00

THOMAS THE RHYMER

"When she approached he pulled off his bonnet and bowed low"

TWENTY SCOTTISH TALES AND LEGENDS

EDITED BY
CYRIL SWINSON

WITH EIGHT ILLUSTRATIONS
BY ALLAN STEWART

Hippocrene Books, Inc.
New York

This edition © 1998 Hippocrene Books, Inc.

Originally published in 1940 by A. & C. Black Ltd., London.

All rights reserved.

For information address:
HIPPOCRENE BOOKS
171 Madison Avenue
New York, NY 10016

*Cataloging-in-Publication Data available from
the Library of Congress.*

ISBN 0-7818-0701-8

Printed in the United States of America.

CONTENTS

Myths and Legends

Tales of Stratagem

Tales of Battle and Pursuit

Kings and Conquests

v

NOTE

Seven stories in this book are by Elizabeth W. Grierson : *Thomas the Rhymer, The Good Housewife and the Little People, The Son of the Strong Man of the Wood, A Mother's Strategy, Iain the Fisherman's Son, Saving the Regalia* and *Kinmont Willie.* Two stories, *The Inheritance* and *The Battle of the Birds,* are by W. J. Glover, and the remaining stories are adapted from Scott's *Tales of a Grandfather.*

ILLUSTRATIONS

By ALLAN STEWART

THOMAS THE RHYMER

MORE than six hundred years ago, there lived in the south of Scotland a very wonderful man named Thomas of Ercildoune, or Thomas the Rhymer.

He lived in an old tower which stood on the banks of a little river called the Leader, which runs into the Tweed, and he had the marvellous gift, not only of writing beautiful verses, but of forecasting the future : that is, he could tell of events long before they happened.

People also gave him the name of True Thomas, for they said that he was not able to tell a lie, no matter how much he wished to do so, and this gift he had received, along with his gift of prophecy, from the Queen of the Fairies, who stole him away when he was young, and kept him in fairyland for seven years and then let him come back to this world for a time, and at last took him away to live with her in fairyland altogether. This is the story which the old country-folk in Scotland tell about him.

One St. Andrew's Day, as he was lying on a bank by a stream called the Huntly Burn, he heard the tinkling of little bells, just like fairy music, and he turned his head quickly to see where it was coming from.

A short distance away, riding over the moor, was the most beautiful lady he had ever seen. She was mounted on a dapple-grey palfrey, and there was a halo of light shining all around her. Her saddle was made of pure ivory, set with precious stones, and padded with crimson satin. Her saddle girths were of silk, and on each buckle was a beryl stone. Her stirrups were cut out of clear crystal, and they were all set with pearls. Her crupper was made of fine embroidery, and for a bridle she used a gold chain.

She wore a riding-skirt of grass-green silk, and a mantle of green velvet, and from each little tress of hair in her horse's mane hung nine and fifty tiny silver bells. No wonder that, as the spirited animal tossed its dainty head, and fretted against its golden rein, the music of these bells sounded far and near.

She appeared to be riding to the chase, for she led seven greyhounds in a leash, and seven otter hounds ran along the path beside her, while round her neck was slung a hunting-horn, and from her girdle hung a sheaf of arrows.

As she rode along she sang snatches of songs to herself, or blew her horn gaily to call her dogs together.

" By my faith," thought Thomas to himself, " it is not every day that I have the chance of meeting such a beauteous being. Methinks she must be the Virgin Mother herself, for she is too fair to belong to this poor earth of ours. Now will I hasten over the hill, and meet her under the Eildon Tree ; perchance she may give me her blessing."

So Thomas hasted, and ran, and came to the Eildon Tree, which grew on the slope of the Eildon Hills, under which, 'tis said, King Arthur and his Knights lie sleeping, and there he waited for the lovely lady. When she approached he pulled off his bonnet and bowed low.

But the lady quickly undeceived him. " Do not do homage to me," she said, " for I am not she whom thou takest me for, and cannot claim such reverence. I am but the Queen of Fairyland, and I ride to the chase with my horn and my hounds."

Then Thomas, fascinated by her loveliness, and loth to lose sight of her, began to make love to her ; but she warned him that, if he did so, her beauty would vanish in a moment, and worse still, she would have the power to throw a spell over him, and to carry him away to her own country. But I wot that her spell had fallen on Thomas already, for it seemed to him that there was nothing on earth to be compared to her favour.

" Here pledge I my troth with thee," he cried recklessly, " and little care I where I am carried, so long as thou art beside me," and as he said this, he gave her a kiss.

What was his horror, as soon as he had done so, to see an awful change come over the lady. Her beautiful clothes crumbled away, and she was left standing in a long ash-coloured gown. All the brightness round her vanished ; her face grew pale and colourless ; her eyes turned dim, and sank in her head ; and, most terrible of all, one-half of her beautiful black hair went grey before his eyes, so that she looked worn and old.

A cruel smile came on her haggard face as she cried triumphantly, " Ah, Thomas, now thou must go with me, and thou must serve me, come weal, come woe, for seven long years."

Then she signed to him to get up behind her on her grey palfrey, and poor Thomas had no power to refuse. He glanced round in despair, taking a last look at the pleasant countryside he loved so well, and the next moment it vanished from his eyes, for the Eildon Hills opened beneath them, and they sank in gloomy caverns, leaving no trace behind.

For three days Thomas and the lady travelled on, in the dreadful gloom. It was like riding through the darkness of the darkest midnight. He could feel the palfrey moving beneath him ; he could hear, close at hand, the roaring of the sea ; and, ever as they rode, it seemed to him that they crossed many rivers, for, as the palfrey struggled through them, he could feel the cold rushing water creeping up to his knees, but never a ray of light came to cheer him.

He grew sick and faint with hunger and terror, and at last he could bear it no longer.

" Woe is me," he cried feebly, " for methinks I die for lack of food."

As he spoke these words, the lady turned her horse's head in the darkness, and, little by little, it began to grow lighter, until at last they emerged in open daylight, and found themselves in a beautiful garden.

It was full of fruit trees, and after the terrible darkness he had passed through, this garden seemed to Thomas like the Garden of Paradise.

There were pear trees in it, covered with pears, and apple trees laden with great juicy apples ; there were dates, and damsons, and figs, and grapes. Brightly coloured parrots were flitting about among the branches, and everywhere the thrushes were singing.

The lady drew rein under an apple tree, and, reaching up her hand, she plucked an apple, and handed it to him. " Take this for thine arles," [1] she said ; " it will confer a great gift on thee, for it will give thee a tongue that cannot lie, and from henceforth men shall call thee ' True Thomas.' "

[1] Money paid at the engagement of a servant.

Now Thomas was not very particular about always being truthful, and this did not seem to him to be a very enviable gift.

"A bonnie gift, forsooth!" he said scornfully. "My tongue is my own, and I would prefer that no one meddled with it. If I am obliged always to tell the truth, how shall I fare when I once more go back to the wicked world? When I take a cow to market, have I always to point out the horn it hath lost, or the piece of skin that is torn? And when I talk to my betters, and would crave a boon of them, must I always tell them my real thoughts, instead of giving them the flattery which, let me tell you, Madam, goes a long way in obtaining a favour?"

"Now hold thy peace," said the lady sharply, "and think thyself favoured to see food at all. Many miles of our journey lie yet before us, and already thou criest out for hunger. Certs, if thou wilt not eat when thou canst, thou shalt have no more opportunity."

Poor Thomas was so hungry, and the apple looked so tempting, that at last he took it and ate it, and the Grace of Truth settled down on his lips for ever: that is why men called him "True Thomas," when in after years he returned to earth.

Then the lady shook her bridle rein, and the palfrey darted forward so quickly that it appeared to be almost flying. On and on they flew, until they came to the World's End, and a great desert stretched before them. Here the lady bade Thomas dismount and lean his head against her knee. " I have three wonders to show thee, Thomas," she said, " and it is thus that thou canst see them best."

Thomas did as he was bid, and when he laid his head against the Fairy Queen's knee, he saw three roads stretching away before him through the sand.

One of them was a rough and narrow road, with thick hedges of thorn on either side, and branches of tangled briar hanging down from them, and lying across the path. Any traveller who travelled by that road would find it beset with many difficulties.

The next road was smooth and broad, and it ran straight and level across the plain. It looked so easy a way that Thomas wondered that anyone ever wanted to go along the narrow path at all.

The third road wound along a hillside, and the banks above it and below it were covered with beautiful brackens, and their delicate fronds rose high on either side, so high, indeed, that they would shelter the wayfarer from the burning heat of the noonday sun.

" That is the best road of all," thought Thomas to himself ; " it looks so fresh and cool, I should like to travel along it."

Then the lady's voice sounded in his ears.

" Seest thou that narrow path," she asked, " all set about with thorns and briars ? That is the Path of Righteousness, and there be but few, oh, so few ! who ever ask where it leads to, or who try to travel by it. And seest thou that broad, broad road, that runs so smoothly across the desert ? That is the Path of Wickedness, and I trow it is a pleasant way, and easy to travel by. Some would fain persuade themselves that it leads to Heaven, but Heaven was never reached by an easy road. 'Tis the narrow road through the briars and thorns that leads us thither, and wise are the men who follow it. And seest thou that bonnie, bonnie road, that winds up round the ferny brae ? That is the way to Fairyland, and that is the road which lies before us."

Here Thomas was about to speak, and to remonstrate with her for carrying him away, but she interrupted him.

" Hush," she said, " thou must be silent now, Thomas ; the time for speech is past. Thou art on the borders of Elfland, and if ever mortal man speak a word in Elfland, he can nevermore go back to his own country."

So Thomas held his peace, and climbed sadly on the palfrey's back, and once more they started on their dread journey. On and on they went, until at last, far away in the distance, a splendid castle appeared, standing on the top of a high hill.

It was built of pure white marble, with massive towers, and lovely gardens stretched in front of it.

"That castle is mine," said the lady proudly. "It belongs to me, and to my husband, who is the King of this country. He is a jealous man, and one greatly to be feared, and, if he knew how friendly thou and I have been, he would kill thee in his rage. Remember, therefore, what I told thee about keeping silence. Thou canst talk to me, an thou wilt, if an opportunity offers, but see to it that thou answerest no one else. Thou must pay no heed to the many knights and squires at court, and I shall pretend that thou talkest in an unknown tongue, and that I learned to understand it in thine own country."

While she was speaking, Thomas was amazed to see that a great change had passed over her again. Her face grew bright, and her grey gown vanished, and the green mantle took its place, and once more she became the beauteous being who had charmed his eyes at the Huntly Burn. And he was still more amazed when, on looking down, he found that his own raiment was changed too, and that he was now dressed in a suit of soft, fine cloth, and that on his feet he wore velvet shoon.

The lady lifted the golden horn which hung from a cord round her neck, and blew a loud blast. At the sound of it all the squires, and knights, and great court ladies came hurrying out to meet their

2

Queen, and Thomas slid from the palfrey's back, and walked humbly at her elbow.

As she had foretold, the pages and squires crowded round him, and would fain have learned his name, and the name of the country to which he belonged, but he pretended not to understand what they said, and so they all came into the great hall of the castle.

At the end of this hall there was a dais, and on it were two thrones. The King of Fairyland was sitting on one, and when he saw the Queen, he rose, and stretched out his hand, and led her to the other, and then a rich banquet was served by thirty knights, who offered the dishes on their bended knees. After that all the court ladies went up and did homage to their Royal Mistress, while Thomas stood, and gazed, and wondered at all the strange things which he saw.

At one side of the hall there was a group of minstrels, playing on all manner of strange instruments. There were harps, and fiddles, and gitterns, and psalteries, and lutes and rebecks, and many more that he could not name. At the other side of the hall a very different scene went on. There were thirty dead harts lying on the stone floor, and stable varlets carried in dead deer until there were thirty of them stretched beside the harts, and the cooks came in with their long knives and cut up the animals, in the sight of all the court.

For three days things went on in the same manner, and still he looked and wondered, and still he spoke to no one, not even to the Queen.

At last she spoke to him. " Dress thee, and get thee gone, Thomas," she said, " for thou mayest not linger here any longer. Myself will convey thee on thy journey, and take thee back safe and sound to thine own country again."

Thomas looked at her in amazement. " I have only been here three days," he said, " and me-thought thou spakest of seven years."

The lady smiled.

" Time passes quickly in this country, Thomas," she replied. " It may not appear so long to thee, but it is seven long years and more, since thou camest into Fairyland. I would fain have kept thee longer ; but it may not be, and I will show to thee the reason. Every seven years an evil spirit comes, and chooses some one out of our court, and carries him away to unknown regions, and, as thou art a stranger, and a goodly fellow withal, I fear me his choice would fall on thee ; and although I brought thee here, and have kept thee here for seven years, 'twill never be said that I betrayed thee to an evil spirit. Therefore this very night we must be gone."

So once more the grey palfrey was brought, and Thomas and the lady mounted it, and they went back by the road by which they had come, and once more they came to the Eildon Tree.

The sun was shining when they arrived, and the birds singing, and the Huntly Burn tinkling just as it had always done, and it seemed to Thomas more impossible than ever that he had been away from it all for more than seven years.

He felt strangely sorry to say farewell to the beautiful lady, and he asked her to give him some token that would prove to people that he had really been in Fairyland.

" Thou hast already the Gift of Truth," she replied, " and I will add to that the Gift of Prophecy, and of writing wondrous verses ; and here is a harp that was fashioned in Fairyland. With its music, set to thine own words, no minstrel on earth shall be to thee a rival. So shall all the world know for certain that thou learnedst the art from no earthly teacher ; and some day, perchance, I will return."

Then the lady vanished, and Thomas was left all alone.

After this, he lived at his Castle of Ercildoune for many a long year, and well he deserved the names of Thomas the Rhymer, and True Thomas, which the country people gave him ; for the verses which he wrote were the sweetest that they had ever heard, while all the things which he prophesied came most surely to pass.

It is remembered still how he met Cospatrick,
Earl of March, one sunny day, and foretold that,
ere the next noon passed, a terrible tempest would
devastate Scotland. The stout Earl laughed, but
his laughter was short, for by next day at noon the
tidings came that Alexander III., that much loved
King, was lying stiff and stark on the sands of
Kinghorn. He also foretold the battles of Flodden
and Pinkie, and the dule and woe which would
follow the defeat of the Scottish arms ; but he also
foretold Bannockburn, where

> " The burn of breid
> Shall run fow reid,"

and the English be repulsed with great loss. He
spoke of the Union of the Crowns of England and
Scotland, under a prince who was the son of a
French Queen, and who yet had the blood of
Bruce in his veins.

It was no wonder that the fame of Thomas of
Ercildoune spread through the length and breadth
of Scotland, or that men came from far and near
to listen to his wonderful words.

.   .   .   .   .   .

Twice seven years came and went, and Scotland
was plunged in war. The English King, Edward I.,
after defeating John Baliol at Dunbar, had taken
possession of the country, and the doughty William
Wallace had arisen to try to wrest it from his hand.

It chanced that one day the Scottish army rested not far from the Tower of Ercildoune.

True Thomas determined to give a feast to the gallant squires and knights who were camped in the neighbourhood—such a feast as had never been held before in the old Tower of Ercildoune. It was spread in the great hall, and nobles were there in their coats of mail, and high-born ladies in robes of shimmering silk. There was wine in abundance, and wooden cups filled with home-brewed ale.

There were musicians who played sweet music, and wonderful stories of war and adventure went round.

And, best of all, when the feast was over, True Thomas, the host, called for the magic harp which he had received from the hands of the Elfin Queen. When it was brought to him a great silence fell on all the company, and everyone sat listening breathlessly while he sang to them song after song of long ago.

He sang of King Arthur and his Table ; he sang of Gawaine and Merlin, Tristrem and Isolde ; and those who listened to the wondrous story felt somehow that they would never hear such minstrelsy again.

Nor did they. For that very night, when all the guests had departed, and the evening mists had settled down over the river, a soldier, in the camp on the hillside, was awakened by a strange patter-ing of little feet on the dry bent [1] of the moorland.

Looking out of his tent, he saw a strange sight.

There, in the bright August moonlight, a snow-white hart and hind were pacing along side by side. They moved in slow and stately measure, paying little heed to the ever-increasing crowd who gathered round their path.

" Let us send for Thomas of Ercildoune," said someone at last ; " mayhap he can tell us what this strange sight bodes."

" Yea, verily, let us send for True Thomas," cried everyone at once, and a little page was hastily despatched to the old tower.

Its master started from his bed when he heard the message, and dressed himself in haste. His face was pale, and his hands shook.

" This sign concerns me," he said to the wondering lad. " It shows me that I have spun my thread of life, and finished my race here."

So saying, he slung his magic harp on his shoulder, and went forth in the moonlight. The men who were waiting for him saw him at a dis-tance, and 'twas noted how often he turned and looked back at his old tower, whose grey stones were touched by the soft autumn moonbeams, as though he were bidding it a long farewell.

He walked along the moor until he met the

[1] Withered grass.

snow-white hart and hind ; then, to everyone's terror and amazement, he turned with them, and all three went down the steep bank, which at that place borders the Leader, and plunged into the river, which was running at high flood.

" He is bewitched ! To the rescue ! To the rescue, ere it be too late ! " cried the crowd with one voice.

But although a knight leaped on his horse in haste, and spurred him at once through the raging torrent, he could see nothing of the Rhymer or his strange companions. They had vanished, leaving neither sign nor trace behind them ; and to this day it is believed that the hart and the hind were messengers from the Queen of the Fairies, and that True Thomas went back with them to dwell in her country for ever.

THE GOOD HOUSEWIFE AND THE
LITTLE PEOPLE

ONCE upon a time there was a rich farmer who had a very thrifty wife. She used to go out and gather all the little bits of wool which she could find on the hillsides, and bring them home. Then, after her family had gone to bed, she would sit up, and card [1] the wool, and spin it into yarn ; then she would weave the yarn into warm cloth, to make garments for her children.

But, as you can fancy, all this work made her feel very tired. Indeed, she was so tired that one night, sitting at her loom, she laid down her shuttle, buried her head in her hands, and burst out crying.

" Oh, that someone would come, from near or far, from land or sea, to help me," she sobbed.

No sooner had the words left her lips than she heard someone knocking at the door.

" Who is there ? " she cried, going to the door and placing her ear to the keyhole.

" Tall Quary, good Housewife, open the door to me. As long as I have, you'll get,"

---

[1] To comb wool so that all the hairs lie the same way.

was the answer, spoken in a strange, unknown tongue.

After some hesitation she opened the door, and there, on the threshold, stood the oddest little woman she had ever seen, dressed in a green dress, and wearing a white mutch on her head.

The good Housewife was so astonished, that she simply stood and stared at her strange visitor ; but without uttering another word, the little woman ran past her, and seated herself at the spinning-wheel.

The mistress shut the door, and turned to go back into the kitchen, but before she had reached it, she heard another knock, and when she went and asked who was there, another queer, shrill voice answered, " Tall Quary, good Housewife, open the door to me. As long as I have, you'll get " ; and when she opened the door there was another queer little woman, in a white mutch and a lilac frock, standing on the threshold.

She too ran into the house without waiting to say " By your leave," and picking up the distaff, began to put some wool on it.

Then, before the good wife could get the door shut, a funny little mannikin, with green trousers and a red pirnie, came out of the darkness, and, following the tiny women into the kitchen, seized hold of a handful of wool, and began to card it, and another wee wee woman followed him, and then another tiny mannikin, and another, and another, until it seemed to the good Housewife that all the Fairies and Pixies in Scotland were coming to her house.

The kitchen was alive with them. Some of them were hanging the great pot on the fire to boil water to wash the wool that was dirty, some were teasing the clean wool, and some were carding it, some were spinning it into yarn, and some were weaving the yarn into great webs of cloth.

And the noise they made was enough to make her head run round. Splash ! splash ! Whirr ! whirr ! Clack ! clack ! The water in the pot bubbled over ; the spinning-wheel whirred ; the shuttle in the loom flew backwards and forwards. It seemed as if she would be deafened by the fray !

And the worst of it was, that they all cried out for something to eat, and although she put on her girdle and baked bannocks as fast as she could, the bannocks were eaten up the moment they were taken off the fire, and yet her uncanny visitors shouted for more.

At last the poor woman was so perplexed that she went into the next room to wake her husband, and see if he could not still the tumult.

But to her horror she found that, although she shook him with all her might, she could not wake him. It was very plain to see that he was bewitched.

Terrified almost out of her senses at this new misfortune, and leaving the Fairies eating her last batch of bannocks, she stole out of the house, and ran as fast as she could to the cottage of a Wise Man, who lived about a mile away.

She knocked at his door until he got up and put his head out of the window to see who was there ; then she told him the whole story.

He listened in silence until she was finished, then he shook his head at her gravely.

" Thou foolish woman," he said, " let this be a lesson to thee never to pray for things that thou dost not want. For thy prayer may be granted, as it hath been granted to-night, and the answer may only bring trouble on thine own head. For before thy husband can be loosed from the spell with which these Little People have bound him, they must be got out of the house, and the fulling-water, which they have boiled, thrown over him.

" And in order to get them out of the house, thou must hurry to the top of that little hill which lies behind the cottage, which some of the country folk call Burg Hill, and others ' The Fairie Knowe.' And when thou hast climbed to the top of it, thou must shout three times with all thy might, ' *Burg Hill is on fire !* '

" Then will all the Fairies run out to see if it be true, for that is where they dwell ; and when they are out of the cottage, thou must slip inside and bar the door ; and as quickly as thou canst, thou must turn the kitchen topsy-turvy, and upset everything that the Fairies have worked with, else if they return before thou hast done so, the things that their fingers have touched will open the door and let them in, in spite of thee."

So the Housewife went away, and climbed to the top of the hillock, and cried three times with all her might, " *Burg Hill is on fire !* " and, sure enough, almost before she had finished, the door of the cottage was flung wide open, and all the little Fairie Folk came running out, knocking one another over in their eagerness to be first at the Hill, and each of them calling for the thing which they valued most, and had left behind them in the Fairie Knowe.

In the confusion the good Housewife slipped down the back of the Knowe, and ran as fast as she could to her cottage, and I can tell you that, when she was once inside it, it did not take her long to bar the door, and turn everything upside down.

She took the band off the spinning-wheel, and twisted the head of the distaff the opposite way.

She lifted the pot of fulling-water off the fire, and turned the room topsy-turvy, and threw down the carding-combs.

Then, when she had done everything she could think of, she put the girdle once more on the fire, and set to work to bake a girdleful of bannocks for her husband's breakfast, for the Fairies had eaten up every bite of bread in the house.

She was busy at this when the Little Folk (who had soon found out that Burg Hill was not on fire at all) returned, and knocked at the door.

" Good Housewife, let us in ! " they cried.

" I cannot open the door," she answered, " for my hands are fast in the dough."

Then the Fairies began to appeal to the things which they had been working with.

" Good Spinning-wheel ! get up and open the door," they whispered.

" How can I," answered the Spinning-wheel, " seeing that my band is undone."

" Kind Distaff ! open the door for us."

" That would I gladly do," said the Distaff, " but I cannot walk, for my head is turned the wrong way."

" Weaving-loom ! have pity, and open the door."

" I am all topsy-turvy, and cannot help myself, far less anyone else," sighed the loom.

" Fulling-water ! open the door," they implored.

" I am off the fire," growled the Fulling-water, " and all my strength is gone."

The Fairies were getting tired and impatient.

" Oh ! Is there nothing that will come to our aid, and open the door," they cried.

" I will," said a little Barley Bannock that was lying toasting on the hearth, and she rose and trundled quickly across the floor.

But, luckily, the Housewife saw her, and she nipped her between her finger and thumb, just as she was half-way across the kitchen, and, because she was only half-baked, she fell with a " splatch " on the cold flags.

Then the Fairies gave up the attempt to get back to the kitchen ; and instead, they climbed up by the windows into the room where the good Housewife's husband was sleeping, and they swarmed up on his bed, and tickled him until he became quite light-headed, and talked nonsense, and flung himself about, as if he had a fever.

" What in the world shall I do now ? " said the good Housewife to herself, and she wrung her hands in despair.

Then, all of a sudden, she remembered what the Wise Man had said about the fulling-water ; and she ran to the kitchen, and lifted a little out of the pot, and carried it back, and threw it over the bed where her husband was.

In an instant he woke up in his right senses ; and, jumping out of bed, he ran across the room and opened the door, and the Fairies vanished, and they have never been seen again from that day to this.

THE SON OF THE STRONG MAN
OF THE WOOD

THERE was once a man who lived in a tiny hut on the borders of a mighty forest. The neighbours wondered that he chose to live there, for the forest was full of all manner of wild animals, some of them timid and gentle enough, but some of them fierce and cruel.

People called him " The Strong Man of the Wood," and the name was well chosen, he was so tall and cheerful and brave.

He was married, and had a sweet young wife whom he loved dearly ; and every night when he returned from hunting, he used to look about for any withered branches which had been blown off the trees in the winter's storms, and he would drag them to the door of the hut, and cut them up for firewood, so that she should have no trouble when the fire came to be lit in the morning.

In this way time passed happily on, until at last a terrible thing happened.

There was a great oak tree growing a little way from the hut, and as no wood burns so brightly as oak wood, the good-hearted man made up his mind that he would prepare a little surprise for his wife by cutting down the massive tree, and carrying home a nice stock of firewood.

But, sad to relate, as he was bending over the root, plying his axe with all his might, the mighty tree bent over and crashed down on him, almost crushing him beneath its weight. He managed to scramble out from under it, however, and with a great effort he raised it on his shoulder, and staggered home with weak and tottering steps.

His strength was quite exhausted ere he reached the door, and when at last he threw down his burden, he fell beside it with a cry of pain.

At the unwonted sound his wife hurried out, and greatly alarmed, helped him to rise and to walk into the house.

" I have received my death-blow," he murmured, as he sank down on the bed. " As the tree crashed over, something within me broke, and I feel my life ebbing fast."

His poor wife tried to cheer him with hopeful words, but he only shook his head, and signed to her to be quiet.

" See," said he, opening his right hand, and showing her a little acorn lying in his palm, " here is an acorn from the tree that killed me. I want thee to promise that, as soon as I am dead, thou wilt plant it on the top of the dung-heap which stands close by the byre door. There it will germinate and grow, and by the time its tiny leaves have pierced through the rubbish that covers it, thou wilt have a little son to cheer thee. He will not be like other children, who learn in a few years to run about and take care of themselves, for thou must care for him and nurse him until he is strong enough to pull up by its roots the tree into which this acorn will grow."

Having said this, the Strong Man of the Wood turned his face to the wall and died, leaving his poor young widow full of sorrow at his loss, and of wonder at the strange words which he had spoken to her.

But, true to her promise, she planted the acorn, and it all came to pass as her husband had foretold. By the time that two tiny brown oak leaves were peeping up above the dung-heap, a little son had been born to her, and, remembering his father's words, she nursed him on her knee until he was seven years old.

Then she carried him out, and, setting him down on the dung-heap, she told him to try and pull up the tender sapling which was growing there.

The little fellow did as he was bid, and tugged, and tugged, but he could not uproot the oak.

" Thou art not strong enough yet, my son," said his mother, and she picked him up again, and carried him back to the house.

Another seven years passed, and the child had

grown into a sturdy boy, bigger by far than most lads of his age, while the tiny sapling had almost grown into a small tree.

" I will try his strength once more," said his mother, so she bade her son run out and try to pull up the young oak tree by its roots.

Alas, alas ! To her great disappointment he failed again. He was strong, but the tree was stronger.

So for another seven weary years she nursed him, and then he tried again. And this time he succeeded, for he pulled the oak tree up by its roots, and threw it down with a shout of triumph at his mother's feet.

" 'Twill make good firewood for thee, mother," he said.

" That it will," said his mother, " and the first use I will put it to is to kindle a fire, and bake a pocketful of bannocks for thee, for it is high time that thou shouldst set out to seek thy fortune. I have cared for thee for one-and-twenty years, thou must care for thyself now."

So the Son of the Strong Man of the Wood put his mother's bannocks in his pocket, and set out to seek his fortune.

At first he walked for many miles without seeing any place where it seemed likely that he could find work, but at last he came in sight of a large farmstead, where there was a stack-yard filled with more stacks than ever he had seen in his life before.

"If all these stacks are to be threshed there ought to be work enough and to spare here," he said to himself, and he went straight up to the door of the farmhouse and knocked.

A waiting-maid came to the door, and she started back in amazement at the sight of the stranger, for the Son of the Strong Man of the Wood was such a big lad, that, in comparison with all the other folk she had ever seen in her life, he was quite a giant.

"What may you want?" she asked timidly, keeping well to the back of the door.

"To speak with thy master, if he be within," said Ranald (for that was the big lad's name) promptly.

The maid-servant turned and ran to the sitting-room, where her master was having his afternoon nap.

"Master, master, wake up!" she cried, "for the biggest lad that ever I saw is at the door, and he is asking for thee."

The master rose and went out, and he too was astonished at the stranger's size. "What dost thou want?" he said, eyeing him from head to foot.

"I want work," said Ranald cheerfully. "I am young and strong, and the man who hires me will have no cause to rue it."

" By my troth thou art strong enough," said the Farmer slowly. (It chanced that he needed help, and this lad seemed to have come just in the nick of time.) " Canst thresh ? "

" That can I," answered Ranald, lifting one of his brawny arms, and swinging it round his head as if it were a flail.

" Well, I will try thee," said the Farmer after a pause, " and I hope that what thou sayest will turn out to be true, and that I will have no cause to rue my choice."

So the bargain was made, and without more ado Ranald asked when he should begin to work.

" Not till to-morrow morning," answered the Farmer, astonished at his zeal, for as a rule his servants were not in such a hurry to begin their work. " There is as much corn waiting there to be threshed as will keep two men busy for six weeks, and after that there are all the stacks in the stack-yard too."

Now at that time farm-servants used to commence their work in the morning when the stars disappeared, and finish it at night, when they once more began to twinkle in the sky ; so before it grew dark Ranald went and peeped into the barn where the men were still at work. He burst out laughing when he saw the flails that they were using ; they seemed to him only fit for pigmies to use.

" These flails are useless," he said contemptuously. "When thou comest here in the morning, thou wilt see the flail that *I* work with."

Then he put his hands in his pockets, and strolled off to a wood which he saw up on the hillside, and when he got there he cut down a young tree, and shaped it into the handle of a flail ; then he walked down the hill again with it upon his shoulder.

When the men saw it they looked at one another, whispering, " What sort of lad is this, for he hath made the mast of his flail as tall as the mast of a ship."

Next day Ranald rose betimes, ere the morning star had quitted the sky, and set to work in the barn. He threshed and threshed with right good will, and his arm was so strong, and his flail so heavy, that before breakfast-time he had threshed out all the corn that was stored there. Then he went out to the stack-yard, and seizing a stack under each arm, he carried them bodily down into the barn and threshed them. Then he went back for another two, and so the work went on, until at dinner-time the barn was full of golden grain, and the courtyard outside was almost buried in straw.

When all was finished he threw down his flail and walked towards the farmhouse, wondering that the Farmer had never come out to see how he was

getting on. Half-way across the courtyard, however, he came upon him, standing still, and gazing
in bewilderment at the empty stack-yard, and the
great piles of straw which were heaped up in every
direction.

" What shall I do next ? " asked Ranald, going
up to him and tapping him on the shoulder.

The master looked at him dully, as if he had
just been wakened out of a dream.

" Do," he said slowly, for he was feeling half
afraid of this new man of his who could do the work
of ten men and appear to be quite fresh when he
was finished. " Thou hadst better go into the
barn and thresh the corn that thou wilt find
there."

" I have threshed that too," answered Ranald,
with a twinkle in his eye, " and now I want to
know what thou wouldst have me do next."

The Farmer did not know what answer to make.
He was feeling more afraid than ever of this
strange servant of his, so he told him to go and get
his dinner, while he went to the barn to see if what
he said was true.

And when he saw that it was all true, his
heart sank within him, and when his eyes fell
on the enormous flail lying in the corner, he
was overcome by terror, and fairly turned and
fled.

" Whoever he is, or wherever he comes from, he

is not canny," he muttered to himself, and he took the back road to the house rather than the front one, for fear he should meet the newcomer, for he wanted to have some time to himself to think how he could get rid of him.

Meanwhile Ranald had finished his dinner, and now he was standing at the front door, and when he saw the Farmer he went across and met him. "And what can I do now?" he asked once more.

"Oh! anything thou hast a mind to," stammered the Farmer, "thou has been so busy all this forenoon, I trow thou hadst better rest in the afternoon."

"Very good," said the big lad calmly, "but ere I go to rest I would fain have a word with thee. Thou hast seen now how much work I can do, and the way in which I do it. But in order to work like that a man of my size needs food, and therefore I must in future have more dinner."

"And how much must thou have?" asked his master anxiously.

"Half a chalder of meal in brose, one day, and half a chalder of meal in bannocks, with the carcass of a two-year-old stot, another," said Ranald quietly.

Then he walked on, while the Farmer ran open-mouthed into the kitchen and began to tell his tale to his old servants who were assembled there.

"Half a chalder of meal in brose, one day, and half a chalder of meal in bannocks, with the carcass of a two-year-old stot, another," they repeated in horror when he had finished his story. "Master, the place will be ruined if thou canst not find some way to get rid of him; for in good sooth he be not human if he can eat all that."

"Get rid of him! That would I gladly," said the Farmer, "but how? If any man can tell me that, I will give him an extra month's wages."

But the servants only looked at one another and shook their heads; but at last one of them spoke—"Send for Big Angus of the Rocks," he said; "if he cannot tell us of a way, no one else can."

So they sent for Big Angus of the Rocks, who was the oldest and wisest man in all the country-side, and when he was come they told him the whole story—about the stacks, and the flail, and, what concerned them more than anything else, the enormous dinner which Ranald demanded.

The old man listened, shaking his head in dismay.

"Alas! Hath he come at last?" he said. "When I was a little boy, and my grandfather was an old man, about as old as I am now, I heard him foretell how some day this place would be ruined by a big giant, and I fear me this stranger must be he."

" But how can we get rid of him ? " asked the Farmer, for he had no wish to let his farm be ruined if he could help it.

" There is but one plan which I can think of," answered the old man. " Set him to open the well in the middle of the field yonder, and order him to dig on and on, until he come to water. He will have to dig deep to reach that, I trow, for I know that the well hath a sandy bottom ; and when he hath gone pretty far down in the earth, let all thy men who can handle a shovel be gathered together on the bank, and let them shovel the loose stones and earth which he hath thrown up, down on him as fast as they can ; so will he be smothered and crushed to death. But hark'ee ! Do it when he is stooping, and if he stand up, let every man run, lest he spring out of the hole, and try to kill them."

That night the Farmer sent for Ranald, and told him that water was getting so scarce that he thought there must be something wrong with the spring, and that, as there was a well in the middle of the ten-acre field, he would like him to open it, so that water could be drawn there.

" Thou must dig deep," he added, " for there is

a sandy bottom, and the water is hard to come
by."

" All right," said Ranald cheerfully ; " I'll
start work on it in the morning.

Next morning the Farmer and his men were
astir early, but Ranald was up before them, already
at work. The Farmer and his men, armed with
spades and shovels, crept up to the hole. Ranald
was stooping down to lift a spadeful of earth.

" Quick, lads, we have him ! " shouted the
Farmer, and one and all set to work to shovel
the earth back into the well as hard as they
could.

But what was their amazement when, just as
they thought they had him covered, he stood up
and shook himself as easily as if he had been shaking
a few flakes of snow from his coat.

" Whist ! " he said, and turned one ear up to
the sky as if he were listening for something.

Then everyone remembered the words of Big
Angus of the Rocks, and they turned and ran for
their lives, in case he should jump out of the hole
and kill them.

Meanwhile Ranald went calmly on with his
work until it was finished. Then he laid his spade
aside, and went home for his dinner.

To his astonishment he found that the door of
the farmhouse was locked and bolted.

He knocked softly, then he knocked loudly, and

at last, as nobody came to open it, he put his shoulder against it and burst it open.

He looked all round for the Farmer, and, to his amazement, he discovered him hiding under the table, shaking with terror. When he saw that Ranald had no intention of harming him, however, he came slowly out, and stood up.

" Hast finished thy work ? " he asked.

" Ay," said Ranald ; " but I was sore pestered by crows while I was at it, for they scratched and scratched, in the heap of earth that I had thrown up, till they sent down dust like to blind me.

" What shall I do now ? " he went on, looking at his master in the most simple way possible.

" Oh, go and get thy dinner ! " answered the Farmer in despair ; and, with a smile, Ranald did as he was bid.

Meanwhile his master hurried off to Big Angus, and told him the whole story.

The old man shook his head. " 'Tis plain we must try another plan," he said, " seeing that the first hath failed."

" But what plan can we try now ? " asked the Farmer.

" Send him to plough the Crooked Ridge of the Field of the Dark Lake," replied Angus. " Out of that came never man or beast alive who ploughed there till going down of sun."

So his master sent for Ranald once more, and told him to go and plough the Crooked Ridge of the Field of the Dark Lake.

" Very well," said the big lad. " I'll begin at star-setting to-morrow."

So in the morning out he went, with his plough upon his shoulders, and leading a pair of horses behind him. When he reached the Field of the Dark Lake he laid down his plough and looked round him.

It was a great bare field, with a high ridge running through it, and one solitary tree growing in the middle of the ridge, with a dark lake lying by the side of it.

He ploughed all day, and everything went well, until, just as the sun was going down, he heard a great splash, and looking towards the lake, he saw a dark shapeless object in the water.

" It is a Monster of some sort," he said to himself, " and that is why my fine master sent me here. Doubtless he hoped it would eat me alive : but if it wants me it must come for me," and without troubling himself further, he went on with his ploughing.

Meanwhile the sun went down, and just as its last rays disappeared beneath the horizon, the huge shapeless Monster came on shore, and crawled up the bank to the end of the Crooked Ridge. Then it began to crawl slowly along the furrow from one end, while Ranald and his horses came to meet it from the other.

They met just under the solitary tree.

" Stand back," he shouted, " or thou wilt see what will happen."

The fierce Beast paid no heed to his words ; but opened his great jaws and swallowed one horse alive.

" That is enough ! " said Ranald in a rage. " I will make thee give that horse back," and letting go the plough, he tied the great Beast's tail to the tree. Of course it struggled, and in its struggles it pulled up the tree by the roots.

" Oh ! ho ! " said Ranald, " just what I wanted," and he picked up the tree, and beat the Monster with it, until the trunk broke into splinters. " Give back that horse," he cried. But the Beast paid no heed. " If thou wilt not give it back, then shalt thou do its work," he said grimly, and he seized hold of it, and yoked it to the plough.

As he was doing this, however, the remaining horse became so terrified at its strange companion, that it broke its traces and galloped home.

The Farmer and his men rejoiced greatly when they saw it coming. " Without doubt the big lad is dead at last," they cried, " the Monster from the Dark Lake hath swallowed him."

But their joy was short-lived, for at that moment

one of them chanced to look out of the window, and who should they see but Ranald coming quietly homewards, while beside him crawled the loathsome beast dragging the plough.

This was worse and worse. With a wild shriek everyone ran to hide himself as best as he might; and when Ranald reached the farm, he found naught save an empty house and silence.

He left the Beast at the door, and strode into the kitchen.

" Where art thou ? " he cried.

There was no answer for a long time, and then at last the Farmer came creeping down the stair from the attic where he had hidden himself, and asked him, in a trembling voice, what he wanted.

" I want to know what I have to do to-morrow," said Ranald.

" Plough," said the Farmer, keeping tight hold of the door that led to the attic stairs.

" The ploughing is all finished," said the big lad.

" That cannot be," answered his master, " there is as much land to plough in that field as would keep two men busy for six weeks."

" But I tell thee it is," said Ranald. " If thou goest out to look, thou wilt not see a single furrow unploughed."

THE HUGE SHAPELESS MONSTER BEGAN TO CRAWL ALONG THE FURROW

" And did nothing trouble thee when thou wert at the job ? " asked the Farmer faintly.

" Oh, nothing but a nasty thing of an ugly Beast that came out of the lake and ate one of the horses," said Ranald carelessly. " I tried to make it give back the horse, but it did not seem to want to do so, so I did not waste time arguing with it, but I yoked it to the plough and made it pull it home."

This was more than the Farmer had bargained for. He crept forward and took hold of Ranald's coat.

" And where is he now ? " he whispered.

" Outside the door," answered Ranald.

The Farmer nearly fell down with terror.

" What didst thou bring him here for ? " he moaned. " Send him away, oh ! send him away ! "

" I just brought him hither to let thee see what manner of Beast he is," laughed Ranald. " Now I will cut off his head, and put him in the great hole behind the dung-heap ; then will we be able to plough the Crooked Ridge in peace hereafter."

He went away to kill the Monster, leaving the Farmer wringing his hands in despair. " Whatever shall we do ? " he said to himself. With a woe-begone face he betook himself to the house of Big Angus, and told him how the big lad had slain the

Monster, instead of the Monster swallowing the big
lad, as they had hoped and expected.

Old Angus could hardly believe his ears.
" There is but one thing more we can do," he said,
" and I cannot but think that it will succeed.
Pretend that all the meal is finished, and say to
him that we can have nothing to eat until he takes
a bag of corn to the Mill of Leckan, and has it
ground there. Tell him he must work all night if
need be, for there is no meal about the place ; and
I warrant that if once he sets his head inside the
Mill of Leckan after sunset, the Big Brownie of the
mill will see to it that he never leaves it again alive.
But hark'ee," added the old man solemnly, " be on
the watch, and if by any chance he *do* escape, for,
as thou sayest, he seemeth to be more than mortal,
take to your heels and run, men, and women, and
bairns."

Once more the Farmer sought Ranald. " The
meal hath run down," he said. " Take the horse,
therefore, and the sled, and a big bag of corn, and
haste thee to the Mill of Leckan. I fear me thou
must grind all night, so as to be back with the meal
in the morning, for there is not so much left in the
barrel as would bake one single bannock."

" Very well," said Ranald, and he went off at
once to yoke the sled.

He arrived at the Mill of Leckan in the gloam-
ing, and as luck would have it, the miller had

locked up the mill, turned his horse out to pasture, and gone to bed. Ranald went to the door of his cottage, and knocked loudly.

" Who is there ? " shouted the Miller.

" 'Tis I, Ranald, Son of the Strong Man of the Wood," was the reply.

" And what mayst thou want ? " asked the Miller.

" I want thee to get up and drive the mill, for I have brought with me a great bag of oats which must be ground ere to-morrow morning."

" For no man on earth will I enter the mill at this time of night," said the Miller.

" But I tell thee thou must," repeated Ranald, " for the folk where I come from be fasting till I take home the meal."

" Fasting or no fasting, it makes no difference ; I stir not from my house till the sun be up," growled the Miller.

" If thou wilt not get up thyself to grind the corn," said Ranald cheerily, " waste no more of my time, but give me the key."

Now the Miller wanted to go to sleep, so he gave Ranald the key of the mill, and bade him begone, adding, that if any misfortune befell him, as it was sure to do, it was his own fault.

Ranald took the key and opened the mill, then he carried in the bag of corn, and, making a fire of reeds and peats, he spread it out on the kiln to harden.

Then he put it into the hopper, and set the mill a-going, and in no very long time some of the corn was ground into meal.

When this was done, he began to feel hungry, which was little wonder, for the Farmer had sent him away in such a hurry that he had had no time to take his supper.

So he made some of the meal into bannocks, and set them down on the hot kiln to bake. In a little while, when they were nice and crisp, and almost ready for eating, he heard a strange rustling in a dark corner, and looking round, he saw a great hairy figure rising up among the shadows, and stretching out a huge paw to seize one of the bannocks.

" 'Tis nothing but a Brownie after all," he said to himself; then he turned and faced his uncanny companion fearlessly.

" Keep back," he said sharply; but the Brownie paid no heed. It only stretched out its great paw farther, and seized one of the bannocks.

" Don't do that again," said Ranald angrily.

The Brownie paid no attention, but helped itself to another bannock.

" If thou touchest another one, dearly shalt thou rue it," Ranald cried in a rage.

But the only answer the creature made was to seize the third, and last, bannock.

" Put them back," shouted Ranald, almost

beside himself with anger, and taking one leap, he seized hold of the Brownie.

Then began a great and fearful struggle. At the first turn the roof of the mill crashed in ; at the second, the kiln fell on the floor, a heap of ruins.

Outside, in his cottage, the Miller heard the noise, and wrapping his head in the blankets, crept to the foot of the bed ; while his wife, with one wild scream, jumped out of bed altogether, and hid underneath it.

Meanwhile Ranald had won the battle, and the Brownie was meekly asking to be allowed to go away.

" Not until thou hast rebuilt the mill and the kiln, and put my bannocks where thou foundest them," answered Ranald sternly.

" Let go thy hand, and I will do it," said the Brownie.

" Nay, but thou wilt do it ere I let thee go," answered his captor. " How am I to know that thou wilt not run away ? "

So with Ranald's hand firmly grasping the back of his neck, the Brownie set to work to put the roof on the mill and build up the kiln.

At last all was finished. The mill and the kiln were just as they had been when Ranald arrived.

" Now let me go," groaned the Brownie.

"Not until thou hast found the bannocks, and put them back on the kiln," said Ranald. "Dost think that I am going to be done out of my supper by thee?" and he tightened his grip on the Brownie's neck.

So the creature had to put his great paw up the chimney, and bring down the bannocks from where he had hidden them, and put them back on the kiln.

"Now thou canst go; and see to it that thou never come back," said Ranald, and, opening the door, he threw the Brownie right out into the darkness. With three terrible shrieks the uncanny creature vanished, and so far as I have heard, he has never been seen from that day to this.

The Miller heard the shrieks, although his head was hidden under the blankets. "Alack! alack!" he moaned, "why did I ever give him the key, for it is clear the Brownie hath killed him."

When Ranald had finished his supper, he ground the rest of the corn, put the meal into the bag, put the bag on the sled, yoked the horse, and locked the door.

The key he carried to the Miller's house; but when he knocked, there was no answer.

He knocked again, and this time he heard a small faint voice, muffled by blankets, asking who was there.

"'Tis I; here is the key of the mill," he

replied. " If thou wilt open the door I will give it thee."

The poor Miller thought it was the Brownie who was at the back of the door.

" Oh, be off ! be off ! " he entreated. " Take the key an' thou wilt, but spare my dwelling."

Ranald laughed a hearty laugh. " 'Tis I," he said, " and not the Brownie, and here is thy key," and he pushed it under the door.

The Miller jumped up in amazement. " *Thou !* " he cried in astonishment. " Dost mean to tell me thou art still alive, after spending a night in the Mill of Leckan ? "

" Ay am I," answered Ranald, " and so wilt thou be if thou hast a mind to try it ; for I have made the Thing that dwells there run away, and I promise thee it will never trouble thee again."

Meanwhile, at the farm, the Farmer was anxiously waiting to see whether his third plot had been successful or not. He had stationed men on all the hilltops to keep a look-out, and give him timely warning should they see Ranald returning. Great was his dismay and disappointment when one of them came running down to say that he saw Ranald in the distance with the sled and the bag of meal.

" He will be here in less than an hour," he gasped, for he was breathless with running, " and then I wot not what will become of us all, for he cannot be so blind as not to see that we are doing our best to destroy him."

" Troth, we will not wait till he comes," said the Farmer, whose evil conscience made him a coward.

And so it came about that when honest, good-hearted Ranald came back with the meal, instead of finding a group of hungry folk waiting for him, as he had expected, he found the farm deserted, and every soul belonging to it fled.

" 'Tis none of my doing," he said to himself, " for I would have served my master faithfully, if he had been content to give me enough to eat. However, I need not grumble, for here is a well-stocked farm ready to my hand, and I will e'en bring my old mother here, and we will live peacefully together."

So back he went to the hut by the forest, and told his mother all that had befallen him, and how he had gained possession of a well-stocked farm, and how she must needs come and keep his house.

But his mother was growing old, and the thought of the long miles she would have to go frightened her.

" I am old and frail, my son," she said ; " journeys such as that are for young hearts and young limbs."

Then the big lad stooped down and put his arm tenderly round her. " Thou nursedst me for one-and-twenty years," he said. " 'Tis my turn now to repay thee " ; and without more ado he lifted her on his back, and carried her safely to the farm ; and there they lived in ease and plenty, and if they be not dead, they are living there still for all I know.

THE INHERITANCE

THERE was once a farmer who was well off. He had three sons. When he was on his death-bed he called them to him and said, " My sons, I am going to leave you ; let there be no disputing when I am gone. In a certain drawer, in a dresser in the inner room, you will find a sum of gold ; divide it fairly and honestly amongst you, work the farm, and live together as you have done with me." Shortly afterwards the old man died, and when the funeral was over they went to the drawer, and when they drew it out there was nothing in it.

They stood for a while without speaking a word. Then the youngest spoke. " There is no knowing if there ever was any money at all." " There was money, surely, wherever it is now," said the second ; and the eldest said, " Our father never told a lie. There was money, certainly, though I cannot understand the matter. Come, let us go to our father's friend ; he knew him well ; he was at school with him ; and no man knew so much of his affairs. Let us go to consult him."

So the brothers went to the house of the old man and told him all that had happened.

" Stay with me," said the old man, " and I will think over this matter. I cannot understand it ; for, as you know, your father and I were very great friends. When he had children I stood sponsor, and when I had children he did the same. I know that your father never told a lie." And he kept them there, and gave them meat and drink for ten days.

Then he sent for the three young lads, and he made them sit down beside him, and said :

" There was once a young lad, and he was poor, and he fell in love with the daughter of a rich neighbour. The maiden loved him too, but because he was so poor there could be no wedding. At last they pledged themselves to each other, and the young man went away and stayed in his own house. After a time there came another suitor, and because he was well-off, the girl's father made her promise to marry him, and after a time they were married. But directly afterwards the bridegroom found her weeping and bewailing. ' What ails thee ? ' he said. The bride would say nothing for a long time, then she told him all about it, and how she had pledged herself to another. ' Dress thyself,' said the man, ' and follow me.' So she dressed herself in her wedding clothes, and he took the horse, and put her behind him, and rode to the house of the other man, leaving the bride there at the door while he returned home.

" ' What brought thee here ? ' said he.

" ' The man I married to-day. When I told him of the promise we had made he brought me here himself and left me.'

" Immediately he loosed the maiden from the promise she had given, and set her on the horse, telling her to return to her husband.

" So the bride rode away. She had not gone far when she came to a thick wood where three robbers stopped and seized her.

" ' Aha ! ' said one, ' we have waited long, and have got nothing, but now we have the bride herself.'

" ' Oh, said she, ' let me go, let me go to my husband. Here are ten pounds in gold—take them, and let me go on my journey.' So she begged and prayed for a long time.

" At last one of the robbers, who was of a better nature than the rest, said, ' Come, I will take you home myself.'

" ' Take thou the money,' said she.

" ' I will not take a penny,' said the robber, but the other two said, ' Give us the money,' and they took the ten pounds.

" The maiden rode home, and the robber left her at her husband's door.

" Now," said the old man, " which of all these do you think did best ? "

" I think the man that sent the maiden to him

to whom she was pledged, was the honest, generous man," said the eldest son. " He did well."

The second said, " Yes, but the man to whom she was pledged did still better, when he sent her to her husband."

" Then," said the youngest, " I don't know myself ; but perhaps the wisest of all were the robbers who got the money."

Then the old man rose up and said, " Thou hast thy father's gold and silver. I have kept you here for ten days. I have watched you well. I know your father never told a lie, and thou hast stolen the money." So the youngest son had to confess that he had stolen the money and hidden it away, for fear his brothers did not give him a fair share. The old man sent him to recover it, and he then divided it equally among them.

THE BATTLE OF THE BIRDS

THERE was once a farmer who worked very hard. He worked from early morning until late at night, and he stopped only when it was too dark for him to see what he was doing, and when the moon was full he would work on all through the night, ploughing and sowing and reaping his crops. But even though he worked so hard, and his wife helped him all she could, there was never time enough to do everything that had to be done.

Every market-day he went into town and tried to find a servant to come and help him, but there were no servants to be had, and try as he would he could not get one for love or money. It made him very unhappy, and one day as he paused for a moment in the stackyard, where he had been busy threshing out the corn since early morning, he could not help saying aloud to himself, " I shall never finish this threshing before the winter sets in. If only I could get a man to help me."

A little wren who had been watching him with interest for a long time, chirped up and said, " Won't you let me help you thresh the corn ? "

The farmer laughed heartily, and the absurdity of the little wren's request put him into such a good humour, that he set to work again with a will. But every time he paused the little wren hopped up and again made her request. At last the farmer gave his consent, and this is where the story really begins.

The little wren hopped off to fetch her flail, and in a short time she was back in the yard ready to start work. At the first stroke she knocked a few grains to the ground, and immediately a mouse came out from under the straw and gobbled them up.

" You mustn't do that," said the wren, as she went on with her work. The mouse took no notice and went on eating up the corn as fast as he could. The wren saw that her words were wasted, so she flew away to summon twelve of her friends to come and help her to drive away the mouse.

When she returned with her friends she found that he had also summoned help, and a long line of mice of all sizes were sitting behind him ready for the fray.

" We shall soon see which side is the stronger," said the mouse arrogantly.

" By all means," said the wren, " but not here. We will fight it out on an open field." So they all adjourned to an open field nearby, and on the way the mice summoned all their friends to help them. Rats and mice, rabbits and snakes, stoats and weasels, all scurried along to join in the battle. And all the birds of the air left their work, and hastened to help the wrens : robins and ravens, seagulls and sparrows, blackbirds and starlings, eagles and owls, herons and bats, they were all there.

The battle was long and fierce, and both sides fought hard for victory. The hours passed by, the sun went down, and the stars came out, but still the fight went on. The noise was so great that it woke the son of the king of Tethertown. He got up and went down to the battle, but by the time he arrived it was nearly over, and only one fight was still on, a deadly combat between a great black raven and a snake, and it seemed as if the snake would get the victory over the raven. When the king's son saw this, he helped the raven, and with one blow took the head off the snake. When the raven had taken breath, and saw that the snake was dead, he said, " For thy kindness to me this day, I will give thee a sight. Come up now on the root of my two wings." The king's son had often found it very dull at home, so he readily consented. He mounted upon the raven, who before he stopped, took him over seven Bens, and seven Glens, and seven Mountain Moors.

THE PRINCE AND HIS BRIDE ESCAPING FROM THE GIANT

" Now," said the raven, " seest thou that house yonder? Go to it. It is a sister of mine that makes her dwelling there ; and I warrant that she will make thee welcome. And if she asks thee, Wert thou at the battle of the birds? say thou that thou wert. And if she asks, Didst thou see my likeness? say that thou sawest it. But be sure that thou meetest me to-morrow morning here, in this place." The king's son got good and right good treatment that night. Meat of each meat, drink of each drink, warm water to his feet, and a soft bed for his limbs.

On the next day the raven gave him the same sight over seven Bens, and seven Glens, and seven Mountain Moors. They saw a dwelling far off, but, though far off, they were soon there. He got good treatment this night, as before—plenty of meat and drink, and warm water to his feet, and a soft bed to his limbs—and on the next day it was the same thing.

On the third morning, instead of seeing the raven as at the other times, who should meet him but the handsomest lad he ever saw, with a bundle in his hand. The king's son asked this lad if he had seen a big black raven. Said the lad to him, " Thou wilt never see the raven again, for I am that raven. I was put under a spell ; it was meeting thee that loosed me, and for that thou art getting this bundle. Now," said the lad, " thou wilt turn back on the self-same steps, and thou wilt lie a night in each house, as thou wert before ; but thy lot is not to loose this bundle which I give thee, till thou art in the place where thou wouldst most wish to dwell."

The king's son turned his back to the lad, and his face to his father's house ; and he got lodging from the raven's sisters, just as he got it when going forward. When he was nearing his father's house he was going through a close wood. It seemed to him that the bundle was growing heavy, and he thought he would look what was in it.

When he loosed the bundle, it was not without astonishing himself. In a twinkling he saw the very grandest place he ever saw. A great castle, and an orchard about the castle, in which was every kind of fruit and herb. He stood full of wonder and regret for having loosed the bundle—it was not in his power to put it back again—and he would have wished this pretty place to be in the pretty little green hollow that was opposite his father's house ; but, at a glance, he saw a great giant coming towards him.

" Bad's the place where thou hast built thy house, king's son," said the giant.

" Yes, but it is not here I would wish it to be, though it happened to be here by mishap," said the king's son.

" What's the reward thou wouldst give me for putting it back in the bundle as it was before ? "

" What's the reward thou wouldst ask ? "

" Give me the first son thou hast when he is seven years of age," said the giant.

" Thou wilt get that if I have a son," said the king's son.

In a twinkling the giant put each garden, and orchard, and castle in the bundle as they were before. " Now," said the giant, " take thou thine own road, and I will take my road ; but mind thy promise, and though thou shouldst forget, I will remember."

The king's son took to the road, and at the end of a few days he reached the place he was fondest of. He loosed the bundle, and the same place was just as it was before. And when he opened the castle door he saw the handsomest maiden he ever cast eye upon.

" Advance, king's son," said the pretty maid ; " everything is in order for thee, if thou wilt marry me."

" I will indeed, and that as soon as may be," said the king's son. And they were married.

But at the end of a day and seven years, to his great horror the king's son saw the giant approaching the castle. The king's son remembered his promise to the giant, and till now he had not told his promise to his wife. "Leave thou the matter to me," said the queen, to her husband who was now king of Tethertown.

"Where is your son?" asked the giant.

"Thou wilt get him," said the king, "when his mother has prepared him for the journey." The queen arrayed the cook's son, and she gave him to the giant by the hand. The giant went away with him; but he had not gone far when he put a rod in the hand of the little laddie. The giant asked him, "If thy father had that rod what would he do with it?"

"If my father had that rod he would beat the dogs and the cats, if they would be going near the king's meat," said the little laddie.

"Thou'rt the cook's son," said the giant, and he turned back to the castle in rage and madness. He told them that if they did not turn out the king's son to him, the highest stone of the castle would be the lowest.

Said the queen to the king, "There is still a chance; the butler's son is of the same age as our own."

She arrayed the butler's son and gave him to the giant by the hand. The giant had not gone far when he put the rod in his hand. "If thy father had that rod," said the giant, "what would he do with it?"

"He would beat the dogs and the cats when

they would be coming near the king's bottles and glasses."

" Thou art the son of the butler," said the giant, and returned in very great rage and anger. The earth shook under the soles of his feet, and the castle shook and all that was in it. " OUT WITH THY SON," said the giant, " or in a twinkling the stone that is highest in thy dwelling will be the lowest." The king saw that this time there was no escape, so they had to give their son to the giant.

The giant took him to his own house, and he reared him as his own son. One day when the giant was from home, the lad heard the sweetest music he had ever heard in a room at the top of the giant's house. At a glance he saw the finest face he had ever seen. She beckoned to him to come a bit nearer to her, and she told him to go this time, but to be sure to be at the same place about midnight.

And, as he promised, he did. The giant's daughter was at his side in a twinkling, and she said, " To-morrow thou wilt get the choice of my two sisters to marry ; but say thou that thou wilt not take either, but me. My father wants me to marry the son of the king of the Green City, but I do not like him."

On the morrow the giant took out his three daughters, and said, " Now, son of the king of

Tethertown, thou hast not lost by living with me so long. Thou wilt marry one of the two eldest of my daughters, and with her thou wilt go home the day after the wedding."

" If thou wilt give me this pretty little one," said the king's son, " I will take thee at thy word."

The giant's wrath kindled, and he said, " Before thou gett'st her thou must do the three things that I ask thee to do."

" Say on," said the king's son.

The giant took him to the byre. " Now," said the giant, " a hundred cattle live here, and the stable has not been cleansed for seven years. I am going from home to-day, and if this byre is not cleaned before night comes, so clean that a golden apple will run from end to end of it, not only shalt thou not get my daughter, but 'tis a drink of thy blood that will quench my thirst this night."

He began cleaning the byre, but he might as well have tried to drain the ocean. After midday, when sweat was blinding him, the giant's young daughter came to him and said, " Thou art being punished, king's son."

" I am indeed," he said.

" Come over, and lay down thy weariness."

" I will do that," he said ; " there is but death awaiting me, at any rate."

He sat down near her, and was so tired that he fell asleep. When he awoke, the giant's daughter was not to be seen, but the byre was so well cleaned that a golden apple would run from end to end of it.

In came the giant. " Thou hast cleaned the byre, king's son ? "

" I have cleaned it."

" Somebody cleaned it," said the giant.

" Thou didst not clean it, at all events," said the king's son.

" Yes, yes ! Since thou wert so active to-day, thou wilt get to this time to-morrow to thatch this byre with birds'-down—birds with no two feathers of one colour."

The king's son was on foot before the sun ; he caught up his bow and his quiver of arrows to kill the birds. He took to the moors, but the birds were not so easy to take. He was running after them till the sweat was blinding him. About midday who should come but the giant's daughter.

" Thou art exhausting thyself, king's son."

" I am," said he. " There fell but these two blackbirds, and both of one colour."

" Come over and lay down thy weariness on this pretty hillock."

He thought she would aid him this time too, and he sat down near her, and he was not long before he fell asleep.

When he awoke, the giant's daughter was gone. He thought he would go back to the house, where he saw the byre thatched with feathers. When the giant came home, he said, " Thou hast thatched the byre, king's son ? "

" I thatched it."

" Somebody thatched it," said the giant.

" Thou didst not thatch it."

" Yes, yes ! " said the giant. " Now, there is a fir tree beside that loch down there, and there is a magpie's nest in its top. The eggs thou wilt find in the nest. I must have them for my first meal. Not one must be burst or broken, and there are five in the nest."

Early in the morning the king's son went where the tree was, and the tree was not hard to hit upon. Its match was not in the whole wood. From the foot to the first branch was five hundred feet. In vain he tried to scramble up ; he bruised his hands and his legs, but he could get no hold on the tree, and he was about to give it up in despair, when he found his love at his elbow.

" Thou art losing the skin of thy hands and feet."

" Ach ! I am ; I am no sooner up than down."

" This is no time for stopping," said the giant's daughter. She thrust finger after finger into the tree, till she made a ladder for the king's son to go up to the magpie's nest. When he was at the nest, she said, " Make haste now with the eggs, for my father's breath is burning my back." In her hurry she had broken her little finger and left it in the top of the tree.

" Now," said she, " thou wilt go home with the eggs quickly, and thou wilt marry me if thou canst know me. I and my two sisters will be arrayed in the same garments, and made like each other, but look at me when my father says, ' Go, choose thy wife, king's son ' ; and thou wilt see a hand without a little finger."

He gave the eggs to the giant. " Yes, yes ! " said the giant; " make ready for thy marriage."

Then indeed there was a wedding, and it *was* a wedding—giants and gentlemen, and the son of the king of the Green City was in the midst of them. The dancing began, and the giant's house was shaking from top to bottom.

" It is time for thee to depart, son of the king of Tethertown," said the giant, " take thy bride from amidst those."

She put out the hand off which the little finger was, and he caught her by the hand.

" Thou hast aimed well this time too ; but there is no knowing but we may meet thee another way," said the giant.

"We must fly quick, quick, or for certain my father will kill thee," said the giant's daughter.

Out they went, and mounted the blue-grey filly in the stable.

"Stop a while," said she, "and I will play a trick to the old hero." She jumped in, and cut an apple into nine shares ; she put two shares at the head of the bed, two shares at the foot, two shares at the door of the kitchen, two shares at the big door, and one outside the house.

The giant awoke and called, "Are you asleep ?" "We are not yet," said the apple that was at the head of the bed. At the end of a while he called again. "We are not yet," said the apple that was at the foot of the bed. A while after this he called again. "We are not yet," said the apple at the kitchen door. The giant called again. The apple that was at the big door answered. "You are now going far from me," said the giant. "We are not yet," answered the apple that was outside the house. "You are flying," called the giant. The giant jumped on his feet, and to the bed he went, but it was empty.

"My own daughter's tricks are trying me," said the giant. "Here's after them."

In the mouth of day, the giant's daughter said that her father's breath was burning her back. "Put thy hand, quick," said she, "in the ear of the grey filly, and whatever thou findest in it, throw it behind thee."

" There is a twig of a sloe tree," said he.

" Throw it behind thee."

No sooner did he that, than there were twenty miles of blackthorn wood, so thick that scarce a weasel could go through it. The giant came headlong, and there he was fleecing his head and neck in the thorns.

" My own daughter's tricks are here as before," said the giant ; " but if I had my own big axe and wood-knife here, I would not be long making a way through this." He went home for the big axe and the wood-knife, and sure he was not long on his journey and in making a way through the blackthorn.

" I will leave the axe and the wood-knife here till I return."

" If you leave them," said a rook that was in a tree, " we will steal them."

" You will do that," said the giant ; " then I will take them home." He returned and left them at the house.

At the heat of day the giant's daughter felt her father's breath burning her back.

" Put thy finger in the filly's ear, and throw behind thee whatever thou findest in it."

He got a splinter of grey stone, and in a twink-ling there were twenty miles, by breadth and height, of great grey rock behind them. The giant came full pelt, but past the rock he could not go.

" The tricks of my own daughter are the hardest things that ever met me," said the giant ; " but if I had my lever and my mighty mattock, I would not be long making my way through this rock also." There was no help for it, but to turn the chase for them, and he was the boy to split the stones. He was not long making a road through the rock.

" I will leave the tools here, and I will return no more."

" If thou leave them," said the rook, " we will steal them."

" Do that if thou wilt ; there is no time to go back."

At the time of breaking the watch, the giant's daughter said that she was feeling her father's breath burning her back.

" Look in the filly's ear, king's son, or else we are lost."

He did so, and it was a bladder of water that was in her ear this time. He threw it behind him, and there was a fresh-water loch, twenty miles in length and breadth, behind them.

The giant came on, but with the speed he had on him, he was in the middle of the loch, and he went under, and rose no more.

On the next day the young companions were come in sight of his father's house. " Now," said she, " my father is drowned, and he won't trouble us any more ; but before we go farther, go thou to thy father's house, and tell that thou hast brought but me ; this is thy lot, let neither man nor creature kiss thee, for if thou dost thou wilt not remember that thou hast ever seen me."

Every one he met was giving him welcome and luck, and he charged his father and mother not to kiss him ; but as mishap was to be, an old greyhound was in, and she knew him, and jumped up to his mouth, and after that he did not remember the giant's daughter.

She was sitting at the well's side as he left her, but the king's son did not return. As evening came on she climbed up into a tree of oak that was beside the well, and lay in the fork of the tree all that night. A shoemaker had a house near the well, and about midday on the morrow, the shoemaker asked his wife to go for a drink for him out of the well. When she reached the well, and when she saw the shadow of her that was in the tree, thinking it was her own shadow— and she never thought till now she was so handsome—she gave a cast to the dish that was in her hand and it was broken on the ground, and she took herself to the house without vessel or water.

" Where is the water, wife ? " said the shoe-maker.

" Thou shambling, contemptible old carle, without grace, I have stayed too long thy water and wood slave."

" I am thinking, wife, that thou hast turned crazy. Go thou, daughter, quickly, and fetch a drink for thy father."

His daughter went, and in the same way so it happened to her. She never thought till now that she was so lovable, and she took herself home.

" Up with the drink," said her father.

" Thou home-spun shoe carle, dost thou think that I am fit to be thy slave ? "

The poor shoemaker thought that they had taken a turn in their understandings, and he went himself to the well. He saw the shadow of the maiden in the well, and he looked up to the tree, and saw the finest woman he ever saw.

" Thy seat is wavering, but thy face is fair," said the shoemaker. " Come down, for there is need of thee for a short while at my house."

The shoemaker understood that this was the shadow that had driven his people mad. He took her to his house, and said that he had but a poor cottage, but that she should get a share of all that was in it.

At the end of a day or two came a company of gentlemen lads to the shoemaker's house for shoes to be made them, for the king's son had come home, and was going to marry. The lads gave a glance at the giant's daughter. " 'Tis thou hast the pretty daughter here," said they to the shoemaker.

" She is pretty, indeed, but she is no daughter of mine."

" St. Nail ! " said one, " I would give a hundred pounds to marry her."

The two others said the very same. The poor shoemaker said that he had nothing to do with her.

" But," said they, " ask her to-night, and send us word to-morrow."

When the gentles went away, she asked the shoemaker, " What was that they were saying about me ? "

The shoemaker told her.

" Go thou after them," said she, " I will marry one of them, and let him bring his purse with him."

The youth returned, and gave the shoemaker the hundred pounds he promised.

When she saw him she asked the lad for a drink of water from a tumbler that was on the board on the farther side of the room. He went, but back again he could not come, but stood holding the vessel of water the whole night. On the morrow she asked the shoemaker to take the lubberly boy away.

This wooer went and betook himself to his home, but he did not tell the other two how it happened to him. Next came the second youth.

" Look," she said to him, " if the latch is on the door." The latch laid hold of his hands, and kept him standing there the whole of one night. On the morrow he went, under shame and disgrace. No matter, he did not tell the other how it happened, and on the third day he came. As it happened to the two others, so it happened to him. One foot stuck to the floor ; he could neither come nor go. On the morrow he took his soles out and fled, never looking behind him.

" Now," said the girl to the shoemaker, " thine is the sporran of gold ; I have no need of it. It will better thee, and I am no worse for thy kindness to me."

The shoemaker had the shoes ready, and on that very day the king was to be married. He was going to the castle with them when the girl said, " I would like to get a sight of the king's son before he marries."

" Come with me," said the shoemaker, " I am well acquainted with the servants at the castle, and thou shalt get a sight of the king's son and all the company."

When the gentles saw the pretty woman they took her to the guest-room and filled for her a glass of wine. When she was going to drink, a flame went up out of the glass, and a golden pigeon and a silver pigeon sprang out of it. They were flying about when three grains of barley fell on the floor. The silver pigeon sprang and ate it. Said the golden pigeon to him, " If thou hadst minded when I cleared the byre, thou wouldst not eat that without giving me a share."

Again fell three other grains of barley, and the silver pigeon sprang and ate that, as before.

" If thou hadst minded when I thatched the byre, thou wouldst not eat that without giving me my share," said the golden pigeon.

Three other grains fell, and the silver pigeon sprang and ate that.

" If thou hadst minded when I harried the magpie's nest, thou wouldst not eat that without giving me my share," said the golden pigeon. " I lost my little finger bringing it down, and I want it still."

" Thou didst, thou didst," cried the king's son, remembering who she was. The guests thought he was mad when he embraced and kissed her, but they did not think so for long. He told them the whole story and how they were already married; and when the priest came he married them a second time, and gave them his blessing, and their troubles were then over.

IAIN THE FISHERMAN'S SON

How Iain killed the Giants

ONCE upon a time there was an old fisherman who lived in Skye, and his name was Duncan. He was very old and very poor, and when he did not manage to catch any fish, he had often to go supperless to bed.

One day, when he had been out for the whole afternoon and had caught nothing, a beautiful maiden, with long flowing hair and a fair false face, rose out of the sea by the side of his boat, and began to talk to him.

" Hast thou caught any fish ? " she asked.

" No," answered Duncan cautiously, for he knew that he was talking to a daughter of the sea, and he feared her charms.

" I will send plenty of fish to thy net, if thou wilt promise me something in return," she went on : and though the old man feared her, he feared hunger more, so he asked her what it was she wanted him to give her.

" Thy first-born son," said the sea-maiden softly.

" Alas," said old Duncan, " but thou askest that which I do not possess, for my wife and I are old, and we have none to come after us."

" What hast thou, then ? " asked the sea-maiden ; " surely there must be something on God's earth that thou canst call thine own."

" I have but an old mare, and an old dog, and my old wife," said Duncan. " I cannot part with my wife, and my old horse and my old dog are scarce worth gifting."

The sea-maiden smiled a wicked smile, then she dropped some grains of powder into the fisherman's hard wrinkled hand, and told him to put a pinch of it into his wife's tea, and into his mare's fodder, and into his dog's porridge. " If thou doest so, within three years all will be changed," she said ; " and meanwhile I will send thee some fish, if thou wilt promise me thine eldest son."

Poor old Duncan hardly knew what she meant ; but as he was very hungry, he agreed to the bargain, and that night he went home with as much fish as he could carry.

Strange to relate, the mermaid's words came true ; for, within three years, three little sons were born to the old couple, and the old mare had three fine foals, and the old dog three fat puppies.

Duncan called his eldest son Iain, and, as the lad grew to manhood, he and his wife were often very sad at the thought that some day the sea-maiden might come back and claim him.

They managed to keep the secret from the boy, however, until he was eighteen years old, and a fine youth for his age ; then, one day, he found his mother weeping, and he would not be satisfied until she told him the reason. When he heard the story he burst out laughing.

" I will go where there is not a drop of salt water to be found," he said, " and I trow the sea-maiden will have some trouble in following me thither." So he saddled one of his father's horses, and set out on his travels.

He had not gone very far before he came to the body of a dead horse lying by the roadside, round which a lion, and a wolf, and a falcon were sniffing hungrily.

Iain wondered very much at this sight, for although all three animals appeared to be starving, not one of them offered to take a bite.

As he approached the group, the lion spoke to him. " Kind stranger," said he, " wilt thou of thy goodness divide this body for us ? "

Iain jumped from his horse, and, drawing his knife from its sheath, he divided the body for them, giving three shares to the lion, two shares to the wolf, and one share to the falcon.

As soon as he had done so they thanked him right heartily, telling him how they were almost dead with hunger, yet they could not eat because they were under a spell, which could only be broken when someone came and divided the body for them : and, to show their gratitude, they all promised to help him, if ever he should need their aid.

" If strength of limb or of fang will give thee succour, mind me, and I will be at thy side," said the lion. " If fleetness of foot or sharpness of tooth will loose thee, mind me, and I will be at thy side," said the wolf. " If thou art in straits where swiftness of wing or crook of claw will do thee good, mind me, and I will be at thy side," said the falcon.

Touched by their thoughtfulness, Iain thanked them all, and promised to apply to them for help when he needed it ; then he rode on.

After a time, when he had put many miles between him and the salt sea, he bethought him that it was time to look for work ; and as he heard that the King of that country needed a cowherd, he went and offered his services, which were accepted.

The King was rather a hard master, and the bargain that he made with his new cowherd was, that he should be paid according to the measure of milk that the cows gave.

The fields round the King's Castle were very bare, and the poor animals found so little to eat the first day, that at night, when they were milked, there was hardly any milk, and the King was so angry he ordered that a very scanty supper should be given to the cowherd.

" There will be no more milk until there be better pasture," said Iain to himself. " To-morrow I must drive my flock farther afield."

So on the morrow he drove the cows in front of him until he came to a fine park, with plenty of good grass growing in it, but the gate was shut. He opened it, and drove the beasts in.

" There will be milk to-night, I warrant," he said to himself, and he lay down to rest, while they had a good meal. Presently a terrible trampling was heard, and when he looked up he saw a great Giant coming towards him.

The Giant was terrible to behold, for he had seven heads and seven humps, and as he walked, he gnashed with all his teeth.

When he came up to the herd of cows he seized six of them by their tails, and throwing them over his shoulder as easily as if they had been rats, he turned to go home.

" Stop ! " cried Iain in a rage, starting to his feet, and laying hold of his sword. He had had this sword specially made for him at the King's smithy, and it was the strongest and sharpest sword that had ever been forged.

The Giant stopped and looked at him out of his fourteen eyes. " Art speaking to me, little Mannikin ? " he asked.

" Ay, by my troth, that I am," answered Iain. " Wilt thou oblige me by putting down my cows."

The Giant laughed contemptuously. " If thou hadst wished to keep thy cows, thou shouldst not have entered my park," he said.

Just at that moment Iain chanced to think of the lion whom he had met in the way, and instantly he appeared, and with one stroke of his mighty paw, felled the Giant to the ground.

" What wilt thou give me if I set thee free ? " cried Iain.

" I have a wonderful white horse that hath the power to fly through the air," groaned the cowardly Giant, " and a suit of white armour that can be made to fit anyone. The horse is standing behind yon bush, and the suit of armour is strapped on its back ; take them, and let me go."

Iain took the horse and the armour, but he thought it would be just as wise not to let the Giant go, so he cut off his head instead.

That evening, when the cows were milked, there was so much milk that there were not basins enough to hold it, and potters had to be summoned in haste to make some more bowls. This pleased the King so much, that he ordered a very good supper to be put before his cowherd, so that night Iain fared well.

Next day he drove his herd straight back into

the Giant's park, thinking that now that the
Monster was killed there was no one to prevent
them feeding there.   But before half the day was
done, another Giant appeared, with the same
number of humps and the same number of heads,
and he seized eight of the cows by their tails, and
threw them over his shoulder.

" Stop," shouted Iain, for the Giant was turning
to carry them home, just as the other Giant had
done yesterday.

" And who art thou that biddest me stop ? "
asked the Giant haughtily.

Iain immediately thought of summoning the
wolf to his aid. The wolf appeared at once, buried
his sharp teeth deep in the Giant's body, and
brought him to the ground, and then stood over
him, sniffing and snarling, as though he would
have liked to have eaten him alive.

" What wilt thou give me if I set thee free ? "
asked Iain.

" I have a red horse that can fly through the
air, and a red suit of armour that can be made to
fit anyone," groaned the Monster, who was no
braver than the other. " The horse is tied up
behind the stable, and the armour is strapped to
his back ; take them, and let me go."

And Iain took them, but he did not let the
Giant go.

That night the dairymaid brought in even more

milk than she had brought the night before, and the potter had to make more dishes.

Next day it all happened much the same. Iain took the cows back to the park, and another Giant came, and he summoned to his aid the falcon, who struck him to the earth with her talons, and he offered him a green horse that could fly through the air, and a green suit of armour, which he took— and killed the Giant. That night, also, the dishes overflowed with milk.

Next day back went Iain to the park, and this time there appeared the most fearsome old Giantess that ever was seen. She was the wife of one of the Monsters whom Iain had killed, and the mother of the other two, and she looked so terrible that at the sight of her all his courage fled, and he took refuge up a tree.

She took no notice of the herd of cows eating her grass, but came right under the tree, and, looking up, said in a deep voice, " COME DOWN TILL I EAT THEE."

" Not I," said Iain, climbing up as high as he could, and tucking his legs underneath him in case she managed to catch hold of them.

" COME DOWN TILL I EAT THEE," she repeated, stamping her foot. " Thou hast killed my husband and my two sons."

Then Iain thought of a way to kill her. " Open thy mouth, then, and I will jump down thy throat," he said, and she thought he really meant it, for she opened her mouth wide, and as quick as lightning he lifted his great sword, and thrust it down her throat, and pinned her to the ground. " What wilt thou give me if I let thee go ? " he cried, jumping lightly down from the tree, for of course he was not afraid of her now.

" I will give thee a silver basin to wash in, and a golden comb with which to comb thy hair, that will make thee, when thou desirest, the goodliest man in the whole world," she said ; " thou wilt find them in my house upstairs in my chamber."

" I'll rid the earth of thee before I go," said Iain, " for it is not safe to leave thee alive," and he cut off her head, and went to seek the basin and the comb.

How Iain rescued the Princess

That night, to Iain's astonishment, when he reached the King's Castle he found everyone weeping and wailing and wringing their hands. He asked the dairymaid what the matter was, and she told him that there was a Dragon with three heads which lived in a great loch just over the hills from the Castle, and in order to prevent it ravaging all the country round about, a fair maiden was given to it every year. The maiden was chosen by lot, and this year the lot had fallen upon the King's only daughter, and to-morrow she must go away alone, and seat herself on the rocks at the head of the loch, and sit there until the terrible Monster appeared out of the water to devour her.

" But it must not be allowed," cried Iain in horror : " someone must accompany her, and kill the Dragon."

The dairymaid shook her head sadly. " Nobody dare," she said ; " he is such a fearsome Monster, and, besides, he hath a charmed life, and no mortal man can slay him."

" Charmed life, forsooth," muttered Iain to himself.

Next evening, when the Princess was sitting, pale and trembling, among the rocks at the head of the lonely loch awaiting her doom, a gallant Knight, dressed all in white, and carrying an enormous sword, came riding through the air on a white horse.

He brought the horse to earth, dismounted at her side, and gently asked her why she looked so troubled.

" Thou wouldst look troubled too, if thou wert waiting for a Dragon to come out of the water and devour thee," sobbed the maiden, and she told him the whole story.

" I would like to see him try to devour thee," said the Knight gallantly. " He will have to face me and my good sword first."

" He will not come unless I am alone," sobbed the Princess.

" Let me lie down beside thee, with my head on thy lap," said the Knight ; " then he will not see me."

So he lay down with his head in her lap, and soon he fell fast asleep, so that when the Dragon did appear she had to wake him.

He jumped up, and, seizing his sword, began to fight with the awful Monster. Ofttimes it seemed as if he would be defeated, but at last, just as his strength was beginning to fail, he succeeded in cutting off one of the evil beast's three heads. Then the Dragon turned, and plunged deep into the loch, shouting as he did so, " We will come to grips again to-morrow."

Great was the astonishment, and great the rejoicing, when the King's daughter returned home safe and sound, and loud were the murmurs of admiration and praise for the mysterious Knight and his bravery.

" We must find the brave Knight," said the King, " and give him the reward that he deserves." But none of the nobles and courtiers knew anyone who possessed a white horse that could fly through the air, and no one had the least idea who he could be.

Next evening the Princess set out once more to wait for the Dragon, but she went more hopefully, for if a Knight had come to her succour once, he might do so again.

And, sure enough, as she sat waiting and watching for the appearance of her enemy, the Knight came through the air once more, only this time he rode on a red horse, and was clad in red armour from head to foot. Everything happened as it had happened the evening before ; the Dragon appeared out of the loch, and after another fierce struggle he cut off another of his heads. Thereupon the Dragon turned and plunged into the loch again, with the words, " The last fight to-morrow."

Once more there was joy and rejoicing when the Princess returned home the second time safe and sound, for everyone felt sure that the gallant stranger, whoever he was, would conquer the Dragon in the end, and that the country would be delivered from its terrible bondage.

At supper-time, in the hall, everyone was asking his neighbour who the mysterious Knight could be, agreeing that there was only one reward good enough for him, and that was the hand of the King's daughter. Only Iain the cowherd was silent.

The Princess, too, was strangely silent, but she was thinking deep thoughts in her heart, and before the meal was over she had determined on a plan by which her deliverer might be traced.

The next evening she was waiting on the rocks at the end of the loch as usual, and, as usual, the Knight appeared, riding this time on a green horse, and clad all in green, and after he had taken his rest with his head on her lap, he jumped up and killed the Dragon by cutting off the last of his heads. Then, as he had done on the two preceding evenings, he jumped on his horse and vanished.

When the Princess arrived home, and the news spread that the dreaded Monster was slain, and that from henceforth all the maidens in the country might live at ease without the thought haunting them that some day the lot might fall on them, people rejoiced as they had never rejoiced before, and everyone asked the name of the brave champion who had done such a mighty deed.

But this no one could tell, not even the King, although he had ordered the whole Kingdom to be searched for any man who would answer the description that the Princess gave of him.

But the Princess herself solved the riddle. " Gather all thy subjects together, gentle or simple, it matters not which," she said, " and let them all pass before me uncovered. For, when my Knight lay sleeping on my lap, I made a little mark with my bodkin on his left temple, just where the hair touches the skin, and I would know him again amid a thousand."

So all her father's subjects were gathered together, and all passed before her uncovered, but, to her despair, not one of them carried the little mark she had spoken of.

"It must have been a spirit, and no mortal man," she said, as the last man walked away from her. "This grieveth me that it is so, for mortals cannot wed with those who come from another world, and, with my father's consent, I would have liked to bestow my hand upon this brave man."

Just then someone noticed that Iain the cowherd was not in the company, and soon the noise reached the King's ears that he was missing.

"Let him be brought, and that instantly," cried the Monarch, for he suddenly bethought him of the marvellous supply of milk that had been got ever since the youth came, and he began to wonder if he were quite as ordinary a man as he looked.

So two men ran off, and presently they came back, dragging the unwilling cowherd with them, who protested that he was all foul and dirty with his work, and not fit to appear in the King's presence.

"We will pardon the dirt, but we cannot pardon thy appearing in our presence with thy head uncovered," said the King; but although he spoke sternly there was a twinkle in his eye, for he noted that not only did the cowherd wear his cap on his head, but that it was drawn down tightly over his left ear.

" Uncover ! uncover ! " shouted the whole company, and, to Iain's confusion, the Princess stepped forward herself and held out her hand for his cap with a triumphant smile on her face ; and lo ! when his head was bared, there was a tiny mark, fresh pricked with a bodkin, just where the hair touches the skin.

" He is my son-in-law and heir to the Kingdom," cried the King.

In the tumult and excitement, Iain slipped away to his little attic room. Quick as lightning he took down the Giantess's silver basin, and filled it with spring water, and washed his face in it, and combed his hair with her golden comb ; and when, in less time than it takes to tell, he re-entered the hall, he had become such a handsome gallant that everyone was dumb with astonishment, and whispered to each other that the cowherd was a Prince in disguise.

How Iain vanquished the Sea-Maiden and came to the Kingdom

So, amid such rejoicing as had never been known in the kingdom before, the King's daughter and Iain the cowherd were wed.

All went well until one day the Princess took a

great fancy to have a dish of a certain kind of sea-weed called dulse, and nothing would please her but that Iain and she would go over the hills to where the blue sea dashed its crested waves high up on the yellow sands, and gather the dulse from the rocks with her own hands.

Iain could not tell her that his father had promised him to a mermaid, and tried to put her off with excuses. She would listen to none of them, and at last he tried to forget his fears, and they set off.

Alas! no sooner had they arrived at the sea-shore, and had begun to gather dulse, than the sea-maiden, looking just as beautiful and just as false as she had looked nineteen years before, when she appeared to old Duncan as he was fishing, put her head out of the water, and swallowed Iain up in front of his wife's very eyes.

The Princess was well-nigh distraught at this calamity, for she loved her husband dearly, and she ran to an old soothsayer, who lived in the neighbourhood.

" Folk tell me thou art a clever harper, Princess," he replied, " and there is nought that these creatures love so much as music. Take thy harp to the water's edge and play thy sweetest, and 'tis strange if the sea-maiden will not do thy bidding."

So the Princess took her harp to the edge of the sea, and, seating herself on a rock, she played as she had never played before, for love lent skill to her fingers.

Presently the mermaid's head appeared above the water, her eyes gleaming with delight. Instantly the Princess stopped harping.

" Play on," entreated the sea-maiden.

" Not till I see my husband," replied the Princess firmly.

Then the sea-maiden opened her mouth, and she saw her husband's head.

The Princess began to play again ; then once more she stopped.

" I pray thee, play on," sighed the sea-maiden.

" Not till I see my husband's body," said the Princess.

Then the sea-maiden took Iain slowly and reluctantly out of her mouth, and set him on the palm of one of her cold, clammy hands. " Now thou canst see him, play on."

Doubtless the creature intended to swallow Iain again as soon as she was satisfied with the sweet strains which came from his wife's harp, but lo and behold, he did but think of his friend the falcon, and in a moment the bird came and lent him its wings, and he flew lightly on shore.

Alas ! alas ! they were not free from trouble even yet, for while he was embracing his wife, who was overjoyed that he should have escaped from this terrible danger, the sea-maiden climbed softly up on a rock behind, and, seizing the Princess with one fell swoop, plunged with her into the depths of the sea.

In great distress Iain in his turn sought the soothsayer, and asked what he should do.

The wise man considered the matter for a moment. " Thou wast promised to the sea-maiden before thy birth," he said at last, " and thou wilt never be safe from her snares until thou hast killed her."

" But how can I do that ? " asked Iain, " for I have been told that neither lead nor steel have any power against such a creature."

" Neither have they," said the soothsayer ; " but there is another way than that.

" Far over yon hill there lies a dark and narrow glen, where a fierce and savage bull hath his lair. Kill that bull, and out of his mouth will come a ram. Kill that ram, and out of his mouth will come a goose. Kill that goose, and out of her mouth will come an egg, and in that egg lies the soul of the sea-maiden."

Iain thanked him and went his way. He walked over the mountain gaily till he came to the entrance of the little glen where the furious bull had its abode, then he thought of his three friends, and in an instant they were at his side.

" I will kill the bull," said the lion, when they had listened to the story of the wicked sea-maiden, and presently a roar of agony was heard, and the crash of a falling body.

The lion had done his part, but no sooner was the bull dead than a huge ram jumped out of its mouth, and dashing past Iain as he stood in the sunshine, took to the side of the hill.

" I will kill the ram," cried the wolf, and off he set in pursuit. He came up to the ram and buried his sharp teeth in the animal's side. As it fell dead a great grey goose jumped out of its mouth, and flew off in the direction of the sea.

" And I will kill the goose," cried the falcon, as she rose in the air, and just as the goose was flying over the rocks by the seashore, she overtook her, and dug her talons into her breast.

Then an egg fell out of the goose's mouth, and, to Iain's dismay, before he could catch it, it rolled over the rocks into the deepest part of the sea.

" What shall we do now ? " he cried in despair, " we have had all our labour for nought."

The falcon sat on the edge of a rock, with her head on one side, and her eyes shut. She was thinking.

" I have it," she said at last. " There is an

otter who hath a nest close by, and in her nest are two cubs. I will go and talk to her."

She pounced down on her nest, and she stuck a claw of her talon none too gently in each of the little cubs.

"Now," said she to their mother, "there is a goose's egg lying deep down at the bottom of the sea there. I will rest as I am for ten minutes. If within that time thou bringest up the egg, well and good ; I will return whence I came. If thou bringest it not, then my talons go deep in thy babies' breasts."

Needless to say, the poor otter dived for the egg without wasting any time, and in a very few minutes she brought it up safe and sound.

The falcon seized it, and without waiting to thank her, flew off with it and laid it at Iain's feet.

He picked it up hastily, and dashed it with all his might against a sharp rock, and at the very moment it broke, the wicked sea-maiden died under the sea, and his wife was restored to him.

After this, nothing but joy and prosperity came to Iain and his bride. They went home to the King's Castle, and as the King was growing old, and would fain rest, he gave over the Kingdom to Iain, who, in his good fortune, did not forget his own kindred.

He summoned his father and mother to his Court, and saw that they were well provided for, and he made his two brothers rulers over part of the country. History tells that he proved a wise and good King, and his people loved him.

THE GOWRIE CONSPIRACY

ONE sunny morning in the month of August, in the year 1600, when King James VI of Scotland was hunting in Falkland Park, Alexander Ruthven, brother of the Earl of Gowrie, came to him with a strange story.

He told him that while he was out riding the day before, he had seen a suspicious-looking man dressed like a Jesuit, behaving in a strange manner. He had stopped the man, and found that he was concealing a large pot of gold beneath his cloak. The man's explanation of how he came by the gold was so unsatisfactory that Ruthven had detained him at his brother's house in Perth until the King should have an opportunity of examining him and taking possession of the treasure.

The King's interest was aroused by this story, and with the prospect of obtaining a large pot of gold he was induced to ride off with Ruthven towards Perth, with only a few noblemen and servants in attendance.

The King was well disposed towards Alexander Ruthven and his brother. When James was but a boy, their father, the Earl of Gowrie, had been condemned and executed, and his estates confiscated. The King, however, when he came into power, restored the estate and title of Earl to the elder boy and bestowed many favours on both.

When they arrived at Perth, they entered Gowrie House, the mansion of the Earl, a large massive building, having gardens which stretched down to the river Tay. The Earl of Gowrie was, or seemed to be, surprised to see the King arrive so unexpectedly, and caused some entertainment to be hastily prepared for his Majesty's refreshment. After the King had dined, Alexander Ruthven pressed him to come with him to see the prisoner in private ; and James, curious by nature, followed him from one apartment to another, until Ruthven led him into a little turret, where there stood—not a prisoner with a pot of gold but an armed man— prepared, as it seemed, for some violent enterprise.

The King started back, but Ruthven snatched the dagger which the man wore, and pointing it to James' breast, reminded him of his father the Earl of Gowrie's death, and commanded him, upon pain of death, to submit to his pleasure. The King replied that he was but a boy when the Earl of Gowrie suffered, and upbraided Ruthven with ingratitude. The conspirator, moved by remorse or some other reason, assured the King that his life should be safe, and left him in the turret with the armed man, who, not very well selected to aid in a purpose so desperate, stood shaking in his armour, without assisting either his master or the King.

Meanwhile, during this strange scene betwixt the King and Ruthven, the attendants of James had begun to wonder at his absence, when they were suddenly informed by a servant of the Earl of Gowrie that the King had mounted his horse, and set out on his return to Falkland. The noblemen and attendants rushed into the courtyard of the mansion and called for their horses, the Earl of Gowrie at the same time hurrying them away. Here the porter interfered, and said the King could not have left the house, since he had not passed the gate, of which he had the keys. Gowrie, on the other hand, called the man a liar, and insisted that the King had departed.

While the attendants of James knew not what to think, a half-smothered yet terrified voice was heard to scream from the window of a turret above their heads—" Help ! Treason ! Help ! My Lord of Mar ! " They looked upwards, and beheld James's face in great agitation pushed through the window, while a hand was seen grasping his throat and pulling him back.

The explanation was as follows : The King, when left alone with the armed man had, it seems, prevailed upon him to open the lattice window. This was just done when Alexander Ruthven again entered the turret, and swearing that there was no

"HELP! TREASON! HELP, MY LORD OF MAR!"

remedy but the King must needs die, he seized on him, and endeavoured by main force to tie his hands with a garter. James resisted, and in despair dragged Ruthven to the window, now open, and called out to his attendants. His retinue hastened to his assistance. The greater part ran to the principal staircase, of which they found the doors shut, and immediately endeavoured to force them open. Meantime, a page of the King's, Sir John Ramsay, discovered a back stair which led him to the turret, where Ruthven and the King were still struggling. Ramsay then thrust Ruthven, now mortally wounded, towards the private staircase, where he was met by Sir Thomas Erskine and Sir Hugh Herries, two of the royal attendants, who with their swords swiftly made an end of him. His last words were—" Alas ! I am not to blame for this action."

This danger was scarcely over, when the Earl of Gowrie entered the outer chamber with a drawn sword in each hand, followed by seven attendants, demanding vengeance for the death of his brother. The King's followers, only four in number, thrust James back into the turret-room for safety and shut the door, and then engaged in a conflict, which was the more desperate that they fought four to eight, and Herries was a lame and disabled man. But Sir John Ramsay having run the Earl of Gowrie through the heart, he dropped dead without speaking a word, and his servants fled. The doors of the great staircase were now opened to the nobles, who were endeavouring to force their way to the King's assistance.

Many were the stories told of the reason for the conspiracy. Some people even said that the King himself had previously taken a dislike to the brothers, and wished to rid himself of them, although no proof that this was so, or any more adequate reason as to why he wished their death was ever produced.

Others said that the Ruthvens had plotted to hold the King captive, and to deliver him to Queen Elizabeth, and that the scheme had the approval of the Queen. No one can tell, and the conspiracy must now for ever remain a mystery. If Elizabeth had indeed plotted against him it was to no purpose, for in less than three years the King had succeeded her to the throne of England, and had become King James the first of England.

SAVING THE REGALIA

I AM an old woman now, and only fit to sit at the fireside and mind the bairns, but while my fingers are busy with my knitting my mind goes back to the days when I was young and active, and thought little of a hard day's work.

I was the hired lassie at the Manse of Kinneff in those days, and a right good place I had, for the minister and his wife, Mr. and Mrs. Grainger, had no bairns, and though my mistress was strict enough in the way of seeing that I did my work, both the master and she treated me more like one of their own than a stranger.

Especially does my mind dwell on the share I had in the great work of upholding the honour of this auld land of ours, by preventing the Southron loons carrying its Crown and Sceptre and the Great Sword of State away to London.

It was in the year 1651 when, one clear September day, as I was washing up the dinner dishes at the kitchen door, the mistress came out to me with her hat on.

" Haste thee, Alison," said she. " You know how lonesome and dowie Mrs. Ogilvie is feeling, shut up as she is in that great barn of a Castle at

Dunnottar. The only strangers who are allowed to enter the Castle are, as you know, you and me, and that because of my ancient friendship with Margaret Ogilvie. For she and I were cronies when we lived in Edinburgh for our schooling, and the friendship has lasted ever since.

" I want to take some hards of lint with us ; I promised Margaret I would bring her some. While I put on my redingote and tie up the bundle, do thou saddle Donald and dress thyself seemly, but not too fine."

It was not long ere we were on the road, my mistress mounted on Donald, with three great bundles, or hards, of lint strapped on his broad back behind her, while I walked barefoot alongside.

Truly our ancient realm had need of God's grace and protection in those days. For the King had fled to France, and the few folk in Scotland who did not want Master Cromwell and his " Commonwealth "—which was the form of government he had set up in England after the Puritans had beheaded our lawful King, Charles I—still wished for a King, so we crowned his son, Charles II, at Scone.

The outcome of that was, that Cromwell marched with his followers to Scotland and defeated the Royalists, as they called the King's men, at Dunbar, and took all the Castles to the south of the Forth.

Now when Scotland and England had been joined together, which befell in 1603, about thirty years before I was born, the King of Scotland, James VI, had gone away to live at Windsor. He had taken all his belongings with him, but he could not take his Crown, nor his Sceptre, nor his great Sword of State. These belonged to Scotland —her Honours, as men called them, for they were the signs that our northern land was still a kingdom, even though she had had to take England as a partner. And they were now at Dunottar.

So if the Honours of Scotland had been guarded before, they were better guarded now. But Cromwell and his Generals were determined to have them—not, so men said, because they were the Emblems of Royalty and therefore sacred, but because they were worth a mint of money.

So an English army had been brought up to Dunnottar, under a General called Lambert ; and as it seemed that the Castle could not be taken by force of arms, this army had just sat down in front of it, allowing no communication with the mainland, thus hoping to starve the garrison into submission and so obtain possession of the prize.

On the day of which I am speaking we passed through the English lines without much trouble. Our hards of lint were examined by a sentry, who opened out one of them and stuck his pike through the rest, in case we had anything hidden inside the soft, white, fluffy stuff.

A little nail-studded door was opened a few inches, just enough to let us squeeze through with our bundles, and bolted and barred with marvellous speed behind us. Once inside the postern, a few turnings and twistings brought us to the great hall..

Ere I could lay down my bundles and remove my cloak, a sweet voice sounded from the gallery that ran round the hall far above our heads.

" Oh, Mary Grainger ! but you are a blessed sight. And is that the lint that you promised to bring ? Come up to my chamber and rest yourself, and give me some news of the outer world. Jean McIntosh, see and look after Alison, and have that lint carried to the store-room till I have a mind to spin."

I wondered that the lady did not run down, as was her wont, to greet my mistress and lead her upstairs with her own hand ; but when I was summoned to her chamber a little later, to show her how I oiled my wheel, I saw traces of tears on her cheek, and from the look on my mistress's face, I knew that something untoward had happened.

But neither of the ladies said anything, and after I had put Mrs. Ogilvie's wheel to rights, and showed her the proper way to handle her distaff, I descended to the great hall again, and sat down to the very frugal supper of a barley bannock and

a morsel of salt herring, which Jean McIntosh had
set out for me in a little recess at the foot of the
stair. I noticed as I did so that Mr. Ogilvie, who
was in command of the Castle, was standing before
the fire, talking in a low and anxious tone with a
group of grave and bearded men-at-arms.

It was plain that trouble of some kind was
brewing, and Jean McIntosh was not long in
enlightening me as to its nature.

" Our provisions here are running low : they
have just been counting the barrels of herring and
the bags o' meal that are left in the dungeon, and
it's my opinion the master may as well deliver
up the Castle, for starvation it will be very
shortly."

" Oh, but, Jean ! Mr. Ogilvie cannot give up
the Castle," I replied aghast, for, knowing the
strength of the fortress, such a termination of the
siege had never entered my head. " If he did, the
Honours would fall into the hands of the English,
and starvation would be better than that." Before
either of us could say more my mistress came down
the stairs. Donald was waiting for us where we
had left him, and after the mistress had mounted we
travelled in silence, till we had passed the English
camp and were well on our road.

" They are in sore straits in the Castle, Alison,"
she said, and in her voice was the least little bit of
a tremble. " No help has come from France, and

the stores at the Castle are running very low. They may tighten their belts, and hold out for another fortnight or even three weeks, but after that the end must come. That is, if you and me, with the help of the minister, cannot find a way out."

"You and me, mem!" I replied in astonishment. "What can a couple of women like us do?"

"I think we could do a lot, Alison," said my mistress bravely, "if we had plenty of courage and nerve, and trust in God. A plan has come into my head, and both the Governor and his wife think it might be carried out. When the time comes, I will be glad of your help, for I know you are both leal and true, but in the meantime say nothing. A rumour may be spread about the country in a day or two that Sir John Keith, youngest son of the Earl Marischal, to whom, you know, the Castle belongs, has managed to get the Honours to France by sea. If you hear that, you can agree with it. They will put two and two together, and think that you have heard it at the Castle—and believe it."

And sure enough, within the next week, persistent rumours began to get about that the Honours were gone, and that George Ogilvie was but waiting to hear of their safe arrival before he gave up Dunnottar.

A few days later Mrs. Grainger came into my kitchen.

"Alison," she said, "we'll away over to

Dunnottar. Put a thick cloak on you, for we'll be wet before we get back."

" Go to Dunnottar ! " I exclaimed in astonishment. " Had we not better wait for a drier day ? "

Then my mistress came a step nearer, and spoke in an undertone. " The time has come when I need your help, my bairn. And the rainy day makes the job easier. I sent a letter to Mrs. Ogilvie, telling her I was coming, and I did not forget to mention that I would need to bring home with me one of her hards of lint. I stated what it was for, also, to finish the pair of sheets for my sister's wedding present. So whichever Englishman passed the letter into the Castle knows the why and the wherefore of my visit."

Then my heart leaped to my mouth, and I saw it all. " The Sword and the Sceptre may go into the lint," I whispered, but not the Crown—it is too big."

" Wheesht, lassie ! " replied Mrs. Grainger, seizing me by the arm and looking round as if the kitchen walls might have ears. " I am going to put on my old pleated redingote," she added casually. " On a rainy day like this, who will notice how shabby and old-fashioned it is ? And under it there is plenty of room."

We had no difficulty in passing the sentries. Apparently my mistress's letter had aroused no suspicion.

It was with great relief also that we found that Jean McIntosh was ailing and in her bed, for we did not trust her, neither did Mrs. Ogilvie.

We passed an anxious hour, pretending to laugh and talk as usual, and to relieve the strain I gave Mrs. Ogilvie a lesson in spinning.

The hard of lint had already been carried down from the store-room, and while Mrs. Ogilvie herself guarded the door, her husband brought the precious treasures out of their hiding-place in a secret niche in the wall and laid them on the table. Oh ! but it was wonderful to see the glittering gold Crown all set with precious stones, and the slender silver Sceptre, and the great Sword of State in its purple and gold scabbard.

Mr. Ogilvie bedded the Sword skilfully in the soft, fluffy mass, with the Sceptre beside it, and teased and pulled out the lint, and wound it round with a bit of stuff torn from an old curtain, just allowing enough of the white fluff to show through the holes to let everyone see what it was I carried.

" That is as good as I can make it," he said at last. " You must keep it partly under your cloak, Alison, as if to shield it from the rain. And may the Lord, in His mercy, prevent any soldier from running his pike through it ! "

" Now for the Crown," he went on, and paused in perplexity. For the Crown was an awkward thing to hide, with its hoops and pinnacles.

But my mistress was ready for him. Lifting up the skirt of her redingote, she showed the Governor how she had folded a shawl above her other skirts, in the folds of which hung a black linen bag, just big enough to hold the Crown.

" It is a simple plan," she said, " yet I think it will suffice. I am more afraid of Alison's burden than my own. If there is no suspicion of any sort they will not think of searching me, and my skirt is so full they will neither see the Crown when I walk nor when I am once settled on Donald's back. As for mounting, I must just manage that the best way I can."

" Now God shield you for brave women ! " cried Mr. Ogilvie. Without loss of time we made our way, attended by our host, through the great hall and slipping out of the postern, began to pick our steps down the muddy ravine.

" Methinks I hear the Crown rattling, Alison," whispered my mistress anxiously, as she slipped on a slab of rock.

" Nonsense, mem," I replied, for my courage was rising once I was out in the fresh air. " How can it rattle when it is wrapped in one of Mr. Ogilvie's finest kerchiefs ? It was but a little stone which you loosened with your foot."

But my turn for fear came when, as we were ascending the path on the other side of the cleuch, I looked up and saw a tall figure talking to the sentry, close to where Donald was tethered. He was dressed differently from the ordinary soldiers.

" 'Tis the General, mem," I whispered, standing still with consternation. " Whatever will we do ? "

" Come on, and for pity's sake don't look as if you had seen a bogle. Leave the General to me. I would rather it were he than one of his long-faced officers. They say he likes to speak to a pretty woman, and for once I'll try to persuade myself that I can play the part."

And, by faith, she did !

What the minister and his elders of the Kirk of Kinneff would have thought could they have listened to my mistress's wiles as she talked to that old man, I do not know. She was just inspired. She spoke to him about many things—about the weather (it was by now raining old wives and pike-staffs) about his rheumatics, and about how he must miss his wife in this cold and inclement climate, and about the best remedies for rheumatic pains.

By the time she had spoken it all, the General had handed her up on her horse, and had set us on our way with a salute and a bow, and a pleasant word of advice that we should change our wet things as soon as we got home.

" Oh, mistress, mistress ! " I said, when once we had passed the soldiers, " how could you do it, how could you think of the things to say ? "

" It was sheer desperation, Alison," she replied

soberly. " The words just rose up in my mind, as if someone had put them there."

Late that night the rain cleared off and the mist lifted, and by one o'clock in the morning the moon was shining brightly in a clear sky. It shone through the windows of the kirk, and was a great help to the minister and me in the heavy job we were engaged in.

For though we had been successful in bringing the Honours of Scotland to the manse, it was not safe for them to bide there. So the minister had decided that no one was likely to look below the paving-stones in the kirk. While Mrs. Grainger watched, her husband and me, with much ado, pulled out the oak boards that held up the pulpit, and lifted two of the great paving-stones which that erection covered. Then, hollowing out the earth and lime below them, we slipped in the precious treasures, carefully swathed in two of my mistress's best linen sheets. Covering them with a pailful of sawdust, and putting down the stones, and setting the pulpit to rights again, we left them to lie there for eight long years until the Restoration came, and King Charles the Second was brought back to his kingdom, and the Honours could be brought out in safety from under the floor and carried openly back to their proper resting-place in Edinburgh Castle.

A MOTHER'S STRATEGY

IF anyone had gone into Edinburgh Castle in the year 1349, they would soon have found that the most important person there was a little boy of about eight years of age.

He was tall and fair, with blue eyes and an open face, and he would have been very handsome had it not been for a large scarlet mark on one of his cheeks. Everyone paid him deference, from Sir William Crichton, the Chancellor of Scotland, and Governor of the Castle, down to the youngest page-boy. But there was one thing that the little boy was not allowed to do, and that was to cross the threshold of the Castle ; for, although he was King of Scotland, "James of the Fiery Face," as people called him, he was really a prisoner.

The poor little fellow had had a strange life. His father, James I, had been a gallant Prince, and a brave and good man, who had spent most of his youth in captivity at the English King's Court at far-away Windsor ; and his mother was an Englishwoman, Lady Jane Beaufort, whom the Scottish Prince had seen from his windows one dewy May morning and had straightway fallen in love with.

When at last he was set at liberty, the marriage took place, and the young couple went away to their northern Kingdom, carrying with them many of the manners and customs of the English Court, where everyone was more refined and cultured than they were in Scotland.

So we may believe that little Prince James was brought up in a happy home ; and perhaps his first sorrow was when his two eldest sisters were sent away to France, where the Princess Margaret, who was only ten, was married to the Dauphin, and the Princess Eleanor, who was still younger, was married to the Duke of Bretagne.

Then, two years before the time we are talking of, still more dreadful things had happened.

His handsome father and his beautiful young mother had gone away to Perth, to spend Christmas there, taking with them their three youngest children, and little James had been left alone in Edinburgh with his tutor.

Perhaps he did not mind that very much, for Royal children in these days were accustomed to being left with strangers. But one bleak February morning terrible tidings came to Edinburgh, and the little fellow heard the soldiers whispering to each other of the awful thing that had happened a few nights before, in the Black Friars' Monastery in Perth. His father and mother had been rudely interrupted by a crowd of armed men, led by a nobleman called Sir Robert Graham, while they were having a little music in their private rooms before going to bed ; and the good King had been ruthlessly stabbed to death, in spite of the brave efforts of one of the Queen's ladies-in-waiting— who belonged to the House of Douglas—to bar the door with her arm.

Then, almost before the poor child realised what it all meant, bands of stern-looking men began to arrive, the Earls and Barons of the Realm of Scotland, who had been hastily summoned to stand by their Boy-King in this emergency ; and with one or other of them came his mother and her attendants, no longer gay and laughing, as was her wont, but stunned and heart-broken, wearing a bandage which the boy turned sick to look at, for he had heard a whispered word that the wound had been made when the Queen threw herself between her husband and the daggers of his assailants. There, too, were his three little sisters, frightened into silence by the hurried journey from Perth, and the poor girl Douglas, with her splintered arm.

And in the midst of all this misery and con-fusion he himself was set upon a horse, and led down the High Street, and under the Netherbow, and thence by the Canongate to the Abbey Church of Holyrood ; while all along the road the citizens of Edinburgh crowded to their windows, or stood in groups at the close mouths, and gazed at him, half fearfully, half compassionately, the men whispering together, and the women, with their little children clinging to their skirts, wiping their eyes, and shaking their heads pityingly as he passed.

And down in the great Abbey Church they had wrapped him from head to foot in a Royal mantle, and held a crown—much too big for him—over his little head, and touched his brow and his hands with sacred oil, and given him a heavy sceptre to hold ; and then all the grown-up, bearded men, who had hitherto treated him as a baby, had knelt before him, and kissed his hand, swearing allegiance to him.

Then once more he was set on his horse, and the procession re-formed, and went up the long street to the Castle again ; only this time the men who stood watching by the way cheered with all their might, and the women smiled at him through their tears, and crossed themselves, and prayed that God and the saints would bless him ; and by the time that he arrived back at the Castle, and was left once more to play with his toys, it would begin to dawn on his baby mind that he was now a King, the King of Scotland.

But being a King did not mean that life would be easy for him. In those days Scotland was divided into two factions, and life was just like a game of chess, and the little King was considered the most important " piece " to play with. So each side tried to get hold of him.

Two men had been appointed to rule in his name, until he was old enough to rule for himself. These were Sir William Crichton the Chancellor, and Sir Alexander Livingstone, the Governor of Scotland.

But instead of helping one another, and working together for the good of the Kingdom, these two men placed themselves at the head of the rival factions, and simply tried to see which could have the most power.

Sir William Crichton lived in Edinburgh Castle, and having got possession of the little King after his coronation, when at first it was thought safest to keep him within the walls of that massive fortress until his father's murderers had been punished, he determined to keep him altogether ; therefore he never allowed the child to pass the outer barrier of the Castle.

On the other hand, the Queen-mother sided with Livingstone, and lived at Stirling Castle, where he held command ; and as time went on, and she saw no prospect of getting her son into her own keeping, she began to seek means to outwit Chancellor Crichton, and get the little boy out of his hands.

So one summer morning, when James was eight

years old, and a well-grown lad for his age, Sir William was astonished to see a party of ladies ride up the High Street on mules, and to be told that the Queen-mother had so far subdued her pride as to come and tender a request that she might be allowed to see her son inside the Castle, if she were not allowed to have his company outside.

Perhaps Sir William had children of his own, and perhaps he sometimes wondered how they would get on if they never saw their mother and were brought up entirely by men, for, much to everyone's astonishment, he gave orders that Queen Jane was to be admitted, and lodged in the Castle, and that, so long as she made no attempt to take the boy away, she was to have him with her as much as she pleased.

So the Queen's mules were allowed to cross the drawbridge, and to deposit their riders with their belongings in the inner courtyard, and the Queen and her ladies settled down for a short visit, and after the first great bustle of their arrival things went on as usual.

That is to say, they went on better than usual ; for the Queen set herself deliberately to make the grim old soldier like her, and she talked so charmingly, and told him such interesting stories of her life when she was a girl at Windsor, that he quite looked forward to the evenings, when her son had gone to bed, and she would come down into the great hall attended by her ladies, and make the supper-table bright with her presence.

Perhaps he would not have liked her so well if he could have heard her, when she was alone with the little King, talking to him of the fair Castle of Stirling where she lived, and telling him of the great park which surrounded it, where men could go out hunting with hawk and hound, and not be confined to a few narrow courts, as he was in Edinburgh.

Then she would take him to one of the low windows that overlooked the Nor' Loch, where he could see the wide Firth of Forth, with the Kingdom of Fife on the other side, and tell him how the Firth narrowed into a river, which wound through a rich wooded plain until it came to the old Castle of which she had been speaking.

As he listened, the little boy would grow more and more discontented with his surroundings, and begin to wish that he too could go to Stirling, and ride about in the park, and learn to fly falcons among the trees.

Then his mother would whisper a plan to him, and he would be only too ready to agree to it, and promise to hold his tongue, and never let anyone know what she intended to do.

The clever woman's business in the Castle was now accomplished, and the sooner she was gone the better ; so she announced to Sir William that, having seen her son, and assured herself of his welfare, it was time for her to depart, especially as she intended to make a pilgrimage to a famous shrine, " the White Kirk at Brechin," in order to pray for the repose of her husband's soul and the prosperity of her little boy, before she returned to Stirling. And to this end she craved a boon of him.

The Chancellor, who had quite fallen under her spell, was only too willing to grant her any boon that lay within his power.

And the boon she asked turned out to be a very simple one.

She only desired permission to take two great " arks," or coffers, with her, which contained some rich dresses and ornaments that she had been accustomed to wear in the bright days before her widowhood, and which had been lying in the Castle ever since.

" It behoved her," so she said, " for the honour of her son, to go on pilgrimage attired as befitted her rank," and Sir William quite agreed with her.

So he promised to give orders that extra mules should be forthcoming to carry the " arks " down to the sea at Leith, where a ship was lying, ready to convey the Queen to the North.

Then he took leave of her with many regrets ; for she expressed her determination to set out very early in the morning, so as to be on board before the sun attained its full strength.

In the Queen's apartments that night there was great activity. The Queen and her ladies had much packing to do. They quickly packed the belongings they had brought with them, and then turned their attention to the two great boxes. They turned out most of the things from the larger and stronger box and crammed them into the smaller box.

Then very cautiously and carefully they made small holes in the larger box, where no one could see them. It was nearly dawn by the time they had finished, and time for them to go. The boxes were carefully loaded on to the sumpter mules, and in the early dawn the little cavalcade rode down the hill away from the Castle.

As soon as they had left the Castle behind they hastened with all speed to Leith. The Queen rode next to the mule bearing the box, and when they hurried on board the boat which was waiting for them at Leith, she directed that the box should be placed on deck and not packed away at the bottom of the boat. With an anxious eye the Queen watched the road from Edinburgh, and a sigh of relief escaped her lips as the boat drew away from the shore.

Instead of sailing out of the Firth, the boat turned westwards and sailed up the winding

IN THE EARLY DAWN THE LITTLE CAVALCADE RODE DOWN THE
HILL AWAY FROM THE CASTLE

Forth towards Stirling Castle. The Queen stayed on deck, and her eyes constantly wandered towards the box. At last, when Stirling Castle came in sight, she produced the key to the box ; the clasps were undone, and then the Queen herself raised the lid, and the Boy-King, who had been carefully hidden inside, leapt out into his mother's arms. The sound of cheering reached their ears and, turning, they saw that Sir Alexander Livingstone had ridden down to the water's edge with all his forces to welcome them.

They rode to the Castle, and the Royal Standard was unfurled on its highest tower to show that the King of Scotland was within. Thirty miles away in Edinburgh, consternation reigned, and Sir William Crichton tore his hair with rage at being outwitted by a woman.

BRUCE AND THE BLOODHOUND

" MY lord," said John of Lorn, " I have here a bloodhound which formerly belonged to Robert the Bruce. It was much attached to him, and was his constant companion."

" That is indeed interesting," said the Earl of Pembroke as he eyed the hound. " If our plans go well to-day we shall catch our man without a doubt, but if we fail the bloodhound may prove useful. Bruce can scarcely hope to elude the scent of his own hound, cunning as he is, so take it with you when we march against him."

On many occasions before the plans of the noble Earl of Pembroke had gone far from well, and times out of number Bruce and his handful of followers had slipped away from the English armies. But John of Lorn was quite certain that he would not elude them on this occasion.

When the forces of the Earl of Pembroke advanced upon King Robert, he at first thought of fighting, but news reached him that John of Lorn was moving round with another large body to attack him in the rear. He thus resolved to avoid fighting as he was so greatly outnumbered, and therefore divided his men into three bodies, commanding them to retreat by three different ways, thinking that the enemy would not know which party to pursue. He also appointed a place at which they were to assemble again.

When John of Lorn came to the place where the army of Bruce had divided, the bloodhound took his course after one of these divisions, neglecting the other two.

Then John of Lorn knew that Bruce must be in that party, so he urged the hound on with all speed. The King saw that the division he was with was being followed, and being determined to escape from them, he made all his men disperse in ones and twos in different directions, thus thinking that the enemy must needs lose trace of him. He kept only one man along with him, and that was his foster-brother, the son of his nurse.

When John of Lorn came to the place where Bruce's men had scattered, the bloodhound snuffed up and down a little, and then left the footsteps of all the other fugitives, and ran baying upon the track of Bruce and his foster-brother. Then John of Lorn knew that one of these two men was Robert the Bruce. Accordingly he commanded five of his men that were speedy of foot to follow hard, and either make him prisoner or slay him.

The Highlanders started off accordingly, and ran so fast that they gained sight of Bruce and his companion. Bruce was wearing heavy armour, and the more lightly clad Highlanders were rapidly gaining ground.

" What shall we do ? " Bruce asked his brother. " They are getting near."

" There are but five of them," his foster-brother replied, " I am ready to do my best." And so they turned and killed all five of the men.

By this time Bruce was very much fatigued, and yet they dared not sit down to rest, for whenever they paused for an instant, they heard the cry of the bloodhound behind them, and they knew that their enemies were coming up fast after them. At length they came to a wood through which ran a small stream, and Bruce said to his foster-brother :

" Let us wade down this stream for a great way, instead of going straight across, and then the hound will lose the scent. If we were once clear of him I should not be afraid of getting away from John of Lorn."

Accordingly the two men walked down the stream for a long way, taking care to keep their feet in the water, and then when they were at a safe distance they stepped out of the stream on the farther side from the enemy, and went deep into the wood before they stopped to rest.

Meanwhile the hound arrived at the stream and led John of Lorn straight to the place where Bruce had stepped into the water, but after that the scent failed him. John of Lorn was well aware that running water does not retain the scent of a man's foot, like that which remains on turf, and when he saw the dog falter, he knew that once more Robert the Bruce had eluded him.   And so he returned to the Earl of Pembroke.

But Bruce's adventures were not yet ended. They had no food with them, so after they had rested for a while, they walked on through the wood hoping to come upon some cottage or house, where they might beg shelter and refreshment.   At length, in a small clearing in the forest, they came upon three men who looked like thieves or ruffians. They were well armed, and each of them bore a sheep on his back, which it seemed as if he had just stolen.   They hailed the king civilly enough, and he asked them where they were going.

" We are seeking Robert the Bruce," one of them answered ; " we want to join him."

" Then come with me," said Bruce, " I will take you to the King ; I know him well."

The man who had spoken glanced at him sharply, but said nothing.   Bruce noticed this, and began to suspect that the ruffian guessed who he was, and that he and his companions had some scheme afoot against him, in order to gain the large reward which the English had offered for his life.

But he said to them : " Come, my good friends, we will go now, but as we are not well acquainted with each other, you must go before us, and we will follow."

"You have no need to suspect any harm from us," said the man.

"Neither do I suspect any," said Bruce, " but this is the way in which I choose to travel."

The men did as he commanded, and after they had walked for some hours, the men suggested they should rest and cook part of one of the sheep. The King was glad to hear of food, but he insisted that two fires should be kindled, one for himself and his foster-brother and the other for their three companions. The men did as he desired, and in a short time the meat was cooked.

They had to eat it without bread or salt, but as they were very hungry and had eaten nothing since early morning they were glad to get food in any shape or form.

When they had finished eating, a heavy drowsiness fell on King Robert, but realising the danger they were in, he asked his foster-brother to watch for an hour or two while he slept. His foster-brother promised to keep awake and to keep an eye on the activities of their companions. He did his best to keep his word, but the King had not been long asleep when fatigue overcame him and he fell into a deep slumber.

When the three villains saw the King and his attendant asleep, they made signs to each other and without a sound rose up and came towards the King. But the King was a light sleeper, and the faint noise they made as they drew their swords wakened him, and in a flash he was up and ready to meet them. Bruce pushed his foster-brother with his foot to wake him, and he stumbled to his feet with sleep in his eyes. He was thus easy prey for one of the villains, who slew him while he was still looking round for his sword. Thus was Bruce left alone, one man against three, and in the greatest peril of his life. But his amazing strength and the good armour which he wore, stood him in good stead, and he killed the three men, one after another.

He then left the spot, very sorrowful for the death of his faithful foster-brother, and made for the place where he had appointed his men to meet him again.

The place of meeting was a certain farmhouse, and by the time he reached it it was nearly night. He went boldly in, and found the mistress, an old true-hearted Scotswoman, sitting alone. Upon seeing a stranger enter she asked him who and what he was. The King answered that he was a traveller who was journeying through the country.

" All travellers," answered the good woman, " are welcome here, for the sake of one."

" And who is that one," said the King, " for whose sake you make all travellers welcome ? "

" It is our rightful King, Robert the Bruce,"
answered the woman, " who is the lawful lord of
this country ; and although he is now pursued and
hunted with hounds and horns, I hope to live to
see him King over all Scotland."

" Since you love him so well," said the King,
" know that you see him before you. I am Robert
the Bruce."

" You ! " said the woman in great surprise ;
" and why are you alone ? Where are all your
men ? "

" I have none with me at the moment," answered
Bruce, " and therefore I must travel alone."

" But that shall not be," said the brave old
dame. " I have two stout sons, gallant and trusty
men, who shall be your servants for life and death."

No sooner had the old woman brought her sons
to the King, than a great trampling of horses was
heard outside the house. They thought it must be
the English or some of John of Lorn's men, and
the good wife called upon her sons to fight to the
last for King Robert. But Bruce heard the voices
of his brother Edward and Lord James of Douglas,
and he knew that all was well.

Robert the Bruce was indeed glad to meet his
brother and his faithful friend, Lord James, and
the force that came with them. Forgetting hunger
and weariness he immediately began to plan an
attack on the enemy. " For," he said, " they

think that our army has been scattered, and can do them no harm, and their sentries, no doubt, will be careless of their duties to-night."

And thus it was. Bruce and his men found the English an easy prey that night, and in the days that followed he was no less successful in driving the English away, until they were afraid to show themselves in open country, and kept to their fortified towns and castles.

THE BATTLE OF BANNOCKBURN

ROBERT THE BRUCE, King of Scotland, had been so successful in driving out the English from his country, that by the year 1314 only one town of importance remained in their possession.

The town was Stirling, and it put up a strong resistance to the Scottish forces; but the governor of the town, Sir Philip Mowbray, realised that unless the English sent strong reinforcements before midsummer, the town would have to be surrendered.

During a brief lull in the fighting he slipped away and hastened to London. King Edward II was not a wise and brave man like his father, and had long neglected the defence of the Scottish possessions for which his father had fought so dearly. And when the English nobles heard Sir Philip Mowbray's news, their anger was roused, and they told the King that it would be a sin and shame to permit the conquests which Edward I had made to be forfeited to the Scots for want of fighting.

Edward thereupon resolved to go to Scotland himself, and he assembled one of the greatest armies which a King of England ever commanded. Troops were brought from all his dominions, including many brave soldiers from the provinces

which the King of England possessed in France—
many Irish, many Welsh—and all the great English
nobles and barons, with their followers, were
assembled in one great army. The number was not
less than one hundred thousand men.

King Robert the Bruce summoned all his nobles
and barons to join him, when he heard of the great
preparations which the King of England was making. They were not so numerous as the English by
many thousand men. In fact, his whole army did
not very much exceed thirty thousand men, and
they were much worse armed than the wealthy
Englishmen. But on the other hand, Robert, who
was at their head, was one of the most expert
generals of the time, and the officers he had under
him were his brother Edward, his nephew Randolph,
his faithful follower the Douglas, and many other
brave and experienced leaders, who had been
accustomed to fight and gain victories under every
disadvantage of situation and number.

The King, on his part, studied how by subter-
fuge and stratagem he might make up for his lack
of numbers. He knew the superiority of the
English, both in their heavy-armed cavalry, which
were much better mounted and armed than that of
the Scots, and in their archers, who were better
trained than any others in the world. Both these
advantages he resolved to provide against.

With this purpose he led his army down into a

plain near Stirling, near which the English army must needs pass through boggy country, broken with water-courses, while the Scots occupied hard dry ground. He then caused all the ground upon the front of his line of battle, where cavalry were likely to act, to be dug full of holes about as deep as a man's knee. They were filled with light brushwood, and the turf was laid on the top, so that it appeared a plain field, while in reality it was as full of these pits as a honeycomb is of holes.

When the Scottish army was drawn up, the line stretched north and south. On the south, it was terminated by the banks of the brook called Bannockburn, which are so rocky that no troops could attack them there. On the left, the Scottish line extended near to the town of Stirling.

Bruce reviewed his troops very carefully ; all the useless servants, drivers of carts, and such-like, of whom there were very many, he ordered to go behind a height (afterwards, in memory of the event, called the Gillies' Hill—that is, the Servants' hill). Then he spoke to the soldiers in this wise :

" I am determined to win this battle and to gain such a victory over the enemy this day that they will have no fight left in them. Let any man who is not prepared to fight with me to the last, leave the field before the battle begins, and let only those remain who are determined to take the issue of victory or death as God shall send it."

When the main body of his army was thus placed in order, the King posted Randolph, with a body of horse, near to the church of St. Ninian's, commanding him to see that no help reached Stirling Castle. He then dispatched James of Douglas, and Sir Robert Keith, the Marischal of the Scottish army, in order that they might survey, as nearly as they could, the English force, which was now approaching from Falkirk.

They returned with information that the approach of that vast host was one of the most beautiful and terrible sights which could be seen—that the whole country seemed covered with men-at-arms on horse and foot—that the number of standards, banners, and pennons made so gallant a show that the bravest and most numerous host in Christendom might be alarmed to see King Edward moving against them.

It was upon the 23rd of June the King of Scotland heard the news that the English were approaching Stirling. He drew out his army, therefore, in the order which he had before resolved on. After a short time Bruce, who was looking out anxiously for the enemy, saw a body of English cavalry trying to get into Stirling from the eastward. This was the Lord Clifford, who, with a chosen body of eight hundred horse, had been detailed to relieve the castle.

" See, Randolph," said the King to his nephew,

" there is a rose fallen from your chaplet.'' Meaning by this that Randolph had lost some honour by suffering the enemy to pass where he had been stationed to hinder them.

Randolph made no reply, but rushed against Clifford with little more than half his number. The Scots were on foot. The English turned to charge them with their lances, and Randolph drew up his men in close order to receive the onset. He seemed to be in so much danger that Douglas asked leave to go and assist him. The King refused him permission. " Let Randolph," he said, " redeem his own fault ; I cannot break the order of battle for his sake."

Still the danger appeared greater, and the English horse seemed entirely to surround the small handful of Scottish infantry.

" So please you," said Douglas to the King, " my heart will not suffer me to stand idle and see Randolph perish—I must go to his assistance." He rode off accordingly ; but long before they had reached the place of combat, they saw the English horses galloping off, many with empty saddles.

" Halt ! " said Douglas to his men. " Randolph has gained the day ; since we were not soon enough to help him in the battle, do not let us lessen his glory by approaching the field."

Now, that was nobly done ; especially as Douglas and Randolph were always rivals in winning the good opinion of the King and the nation.

The van of the English army now came in sight, and a number of their bravest knights drew near to see what the Scots were doing. They saw King Robert dressed in his armour, and distinguished by a gold crown, which he wore over his helmet.

He was not mounted on his great war-horse, because he did not expect to fight that evening. But he rode on a little pony up and down the ranks of his army, putting his men in order, and carried in his hand a sort of battle-axe made of steel. When the King saw the English horsemen draw near, he advanced a little before his own men, that he might look at them more nearly.

There was a knight among the English, called Sir Henry de Bohun, who thought this would be a good opportunity to gain great fame to himself, and put an end to the war, by killing King Robert. The King being poorly mounted and having no lance, Bohun galloped on him suddenly and furiously, thinking, with his long spear and his tall, powerful horse, easily to bear him down to the ground.

King Robert saw him, and permitted him to come very near, then suddenly turned his pony a little to one side, so that Sir Henry missed him with the lance-point and was in the act of being carried past him by the speed of his horse.

But as he passed, King Robert rose up in his stirrups, and struck Sir Henry on the head with his battle-axe so terrible a blow that it broke to pieces his iron helmet as if it had been a nut-shell, and hurled him from his saddle. He was dead before he reached the ground.

This gallant action was blamed by the Scottish leaders, who thought Bruce ought not to have exposed himself to so much danger when the safety of the whole army depended on him. The King only kept looking at his weapon, which was injured by the force of the blow, and said, " I have broken my good battle-axe."

The next morning, the 24th June, the battle began in terrible earnest at break of day.

The English as they advanced saw the Scots getting into line. The Abbot of Inchaffray walked through their ranks barefooted, and exhorted them to fight for their freedom. They kneeled down as he passed, and prayed to Heaven for victory. King Edward, who saw this, called out, " They kneel down—they are asking forgiveness."

" Yes," said a celebrated English baron, called Ingelram de Umphraville, " but they ask it from God, not from us ; these men will conquer, or die upon the field."

The English King ordered his men to begin the

KING ROBERT ROSE IN HIS STIRRUPS AND STRUCK SIR HENRY DE BOHUN ON THE HEAD
WITH HIS BATTLE-AXE

battle. The archers then bent their bows and
began to shoot so closely together that the arrows
fell like flakes of snow on a Christmas Day.   They
killed many of the Scots, and might, as at Falkirk
and other places, have decided the victory ; but
Bruce was prepared for them.

He had in readiness a body of men-at-arms,
well mounted, who rode at full gallop among the
archers, and as they had no weapons save their
bows and arrows, which they could not use when
they were attacked hand to hand, they were cut
down in great numbers by the Scottish horsemen,
and thrown into total confusion.

The fine English cavalry then advanced to
support their archers, and to attack the Scottish
line. But coming over the ground which was dug
full of pits, the horses fell into these holes, and the
riders lay tumbling about, without any means of
defence, and unable to rise because of the weight
of their armour. The Englishmen began to fall
into general disorder ; and the Scottish King,
bringing up more of his forces, attacked and pressed
them still more closely.

On a sudden, while the battle was obstinately
maintained on both sides, an event happened
which decided the victory. When the servants and
attendants of the Scottish camp, who had been
sent behind the army to the place afterwards called
the Gillies' Hill, saw that their masters were likely

to gain the day, they rushed from their place of concealment with such weapons as they could get, that they might have their share in the victory and in the spoil. The English, seeing them come suddenly over the hill, mistook this disorderly rabble for another army coming to sustain the Scots, and losing all heart, began to shift every man for himself. Edward left the field as fast as he could ride.

Edward first fled to Stirling Castle and entreated admittance ; but Sir Philip Mowbray, the governor, reminded him that he was obliged to surrender the castle next day, so Edward was forced to ride on, closely pursued by Douglas with a body of cavalry.

Douglas continued the chase, not giving King Edward time to alight from horseback even for an instant, and followed him as far as Dunbar, where the English still had a friend in the governor, Patrick, Earl of March. The earl received Edward in his forlorn condition, and furnished him with a fishing skiff, or small ship, in which he escaped to England, having entirely lost his fine army and a great number of his bravest nobles.

The English never before or afterwards lost so dreadful a battle as that of Bannockburn, nor did the Scots ever gain one of the same importance.

FROM TRIUMPH TO DISASTER

ON the 8th July 1745, Prince Charles Edward, the Young Pretender, set sail from France on his gallant attempt to win back the throne of Scotland for the house of Stewart. There is no space to tell here of the triumphs and disappointments of the expedition, and the story of his adventures, his escapes, and his disguises would fill many volumes.

His attempt to win the throne found little support at first. Indeed the Scottish chiefs who met him on his arrival told him that the enterprise was rash to the verge of insanity. The Prince argued with them, but his arguments were of no avail, and they refused to join him, all except one young Highlander who had fallen under the spell of the Prince's charm. The Prince turned to him :

" You at least will not desert me," he said.

" I will follow you to death," the Highlander answered, " were there no other to draw his sword in your cause."

The chiefs caught the enthusiasm of the young man and declared that since the Prince was determined, they would no longer hold back and would join him with all their men.

It was the same everywhere he went, the Prince's enthusiasm for his cause was infectious, and his personal charm irresistible. The brother of Cameron of Lochiel advised him to write to the Prince—" for," he said, " if you trust yourself within the fascination of his presence you will be unable to refuse his requests." And indeed it was so. Lochiel saw the Prince and was persuaded to join him, and with him came many other powerful chiefs.

Thus was the rebellion started, and many are the tales that are told of the seven months that followed. The Prince defeated King George's troops at Prestonpans. He marched into Edinburgh in triumph, and took up his residence at the palace of Holyrood. His popularity increased from day to day, recruits flocked to join him, and he marched into England full of confidence.

His forces reached Derby before he realised that in England, at anyrate, his cause was hopeless. The army returned to Scotland, and at first they were still successful against King George's troops. But as fresh reinforcements reached the English, the tide turned, and at the battle of Culloden the Prince's forces received a decisive defeat, and an end was put for ever to the hopes of Prince Charles Edward and his family.

The Prince fled with a handful of supporters to the fastness of the Highlands, pursued by the

English. A reward of £30,000 was offered for the capture of the Prince. Indeed it was imagined that in a country as poor as the Highlands, a much smaller sum would have ensured the capture of the Prince to the throne, but it was not so.

He was driven from place to place, till he gained South Uist, where he was received by Clanranald, one of the chiefs who had told him of the folly of his expedition on his arrival a few months before. Here for safety he was lodged in a forester's hut of a most miserable kind.

Meanwhile, every lurking-place where the Prince could be hiding was closely watched, and the Western Islands in particular were strictly searched by General Macdonald of the King's army, accompanied by two thousand men. While they were searching with eagerness the interior of the island, its shores were surrounded by small vessels of war, armed boats, and such-like.

It seemed as if the Prince's escape were almost impossible, but the high spirit of a noble-minded woman rescued him when other means had failed. This was the celebrated Flora Macdonald, who chanced to be on a visit to the chief's house. Her stepfather was an enemy of the Prince, and was in command of the Macdonalds who were searching for him on the island, but this did not daunt the courageous woman.

In spite of the danger, Flora Macdonald readily

engaged in a plan for rescuing the unfortunate wanderer. She procured from her stepfather a passport for herself, a man-servant, and a female servant who was termed Betty Burke. She persuaded the Prince to take the part of Betty Burke, and he dressed himself in the garments of a maid, and with the hood of the cloak pulled closely over his head, he passed within a few yards of the Redcoats who were scouring every inch of the island.

That night under cover of darkness Flora Macdonald rowed the prince across to the island of Skye, but even here he was safe for no length of time, and narrowly escaped being taken. A number of troops were searching for him in the district, and soon the wanderer and his guide found themselves within a line of sentinels who closed in round them. After remaining two days cooped up within the hostile circle, without daring to light a fire or to cook any provisions, they at last escaped by creeping down a narrow ravine which divided the posts of the sentinels.

Proceeding in this precarious manner, his clothes tattered, often without food, fire, or shelter, the unfortunate Prince, upheld only by the hope of hearing of a French vessel on the coast, at last reached the mountains of Strathglass, and was compelled to seek refuge in a cave where seven outlaws had taken up their abode. These men

BONNIE PRINCE CHARLIE IN ONE OF HIS HIDING-PLACES

recognising the Prince even in the miserable condition that he was then in, vowed unalterable devotion to his cause. Among the flower of the nation never did a Prince receive more ready and faithful assistance than he did from these poor men.

They rendered him all the assistance in their power, and by craft and cunning procured him a change of dress, clean linen, and food, and went out and obtained valuable information concerning the movements of the troops. Prince Charles Edward remained with these men for about three weeks, and it was with the utmost reluctance that they would permit him to leave them.

" Stay with us," they said, " for the mountains of gold which the government has set upon your head, some gentlemen may betray you. For he could go to some distant country and live upon the price of his dishonour, but to us there exists no such temptation. We can speak no language but our own ; we can live nowhere but in this country, where, were we to injure a hair of your head, the very mountains would fall down to crush us to death."

At last the Prince received news that two French frigates had arrived to carry him to France, and with a few other fugitives he set sail about the 18th of September 1746. His short but brilliant expedition had attracted the attention and admiration of all Europe, for he had been engaged in the most precarious and perilous series of flights, concealments, and escapes that have ever been narrated in history or romance.

During his wanderings the secret of the Prince's concealment was entrusted to hundreds of men and women of every age and rank, but no individual was found, in high or low degree, who thought for an instant of obtaining the heavy ransom for his capture. Such conduct will reflect honour on the Highlands of Scotland while their mountains continue to exist.

THE STORY OF MACBETH

ABOUT the year 1033 there was a King of Scotland called Duncan, a very good old man, and he had two sons, Malcolm and Donaldbane. At this time Scotland was much harassed by the Danes, who landed with their soldiers, took what spoil they could find, burned the houses and buildings, and then got on board, hoisted sails, and hastened away.

Now it happened in King Duncan's time that a great fleet of these Danes came to Scotland and landed their men in Fife. A large Scottish army was raised to fight against them, but as the King was too old to command his army and his sons were too young, he sent one of his near relations, Macbeth.

Macbeth was the son of the Thane of Glammis, and he was a brave soldier. He put himself at the head of the Scottish army and marched against the Danes, and with him went another brave man, Banquo, Thane of Lochaber. A great battle was fought, and Macbeth and Banquo defeated the Danes and drove them back to their ships, leaving a great many of their soldiers both killed and wounded. Then Macbeth and his victorious army marched back to Forres, in the north of Scotland.

There lived at this time in the town of Forres three old women, whom people looked upon as witches, and believed could foretell the future. Even great men, like Macbeth, believed that such persons as these witches of Forres could tell what was to come. The three old women went up to a great moor near Forres and waited by the wayside until Macbeth came by. And then, stepping in front of him as he was marching at the head of his soldiers, the first woman said, " All hail, Macbeth —hail to thee, Thane of Glammis."

And the second woman said, " All hail, Macbeth, hail to thee, Thane of Cawdor."

The third woman came forward and cried, " All hail, Macbeth, that shall be King of Scotland."

Before Macbeth had recovered from his surprise, a messenger came forward to tell him that his father was dead. So he had become Thane of Glammis.

Then another messenger came bearing news from the King, to thank Macbeth for his great victory over the Danes and to tell him that the Thane of Cawdor had rebelled against the King, who had taken his office from him and conferred it on Macbeth. Thus Macbeth became Thane of Cawdor as well as of Glammis, and two of the old womens' promises had been fulfilled. Thus did

Macbeth begin to think how he was to bring the rest to pass and make himself king as well.

Now his wife was a very wicked and ambitious woman. She encouraged him, by every means in her power, and persuaded him that the only way to get possession of the crown was to kill the good old King.

Macbeth was very unwilling to commit so great a crime, but at last, through the wicked advice of his wife and the prophecy of the old women haunting him, Macbeth was tempted to plan the murder of his King and friend. So he invited Duncan to visit him at his castle near Inverness. Macbeth and his lady received the King and all his retinue with much appearance of joy, and made a great feast of welcome.

About the middle of the night the King desired to go to his apartment, and Macbeth conducted him to a fine room which had been prepared for him.

Now it was the custom in those barbarous times for two armed men to guard the door of the chamber where the King slept. Lady Macbeth knew of this custom, and earlier in the evening she had sought out the two watchmen, and plied them with wine which she had secretly drugged, so that when the men went to the King's apartment they were heavy with sleep, and as soon as the King had retired to rest they both fell asleep and slept so soundly that nothing could awaken them. A heavy storm raged throughout the night, yet the noise of the wind and of the thunder did not waken the King, for he was old and weary with his journey. Neither did it waken the two guards from their drunken slumber.

Macbeth did not sleep that night, and in an agony of mind sought to quell the doubts that made him falter in his guilty purpose. If the King was to die, he must die that night. Lady Macbeth, seeing his uncertainty, taunted him with cowardice, and said that she herself, though but a woman, would do the deed if his courage failed him. With these taunts in his ears, Macbeth made his way down the long corridors leading to the King's apartments.

He seized the two dirks from the belts of the sleeping sentinels, and rushing into the inner room stabbed old King Duncan to the heart. Then Macbeth put the blood-stained daggers into the sentinels' hands, and daubed their faces with blood, so that it might appear they had committed the murder.

In the morning the nobles and gentlemen who attended the King assembled in the great hall of the castle, and while they waited talked of the dreadful storm that had raged through the night. Still Duncan did not appear, and at length it was decided that one of the noblemen should go to seek him. With the usual ceremony he approached the inner chamber ; there lay Duncan stiff and cold, and near him, still sleeping, lay the two guards with their blood-stained dirks beside them. The alarum bell was sounded, and loud was the uproar in the castle when the nobles beheld the scene of horror. Macbeth, seemingly more enraged than any, drew his sword, and before anyone could prevent him slew the two guards as they slept, declaring to all present that their guilt deserved immediate punishment.

When Malcolm and Donaldbane, the two sons of the King, saw their father slain in this strange manner within Macbeth's castle, they were afraid, and fled away out of Scotland. Donaldbane flew into some distant islands, but Malcolm went to the Court of the English king, to beg for assistance to place him on the throne as his father's successor.

Macbeth took possession of the kingdom of Scotland, and thus all his wicked wishes seemed to be fulfilled. But he was not happy. He began to reflect how wicked he had been, and how some other person, as ambitious as himself, might do the same thing to him. And for no other reason than the guilty thoughts that preyed on his mind he grew suspicious of Banquo, and he planned his murder.

But this did not make him more happy. He

knew that men had begun to suspect the wicked deeds he had done, and he was constantly afraid that someone would put him to death, or that Malcolm would obtain assistance from England and make war against him.

So he decided to go again to the old women, whose words had first put into his mind the desire to become King, and ask them to foretell his future. The witches told him that he would not be conquered or lose his crown until a great forest, called Birnam Wood, should come to the strong castle called Dunsinane, where Macbeth usually resided. Now Birnam Wood was twelve miles from Dunsinane, and Macbeth thought that it fanwas tastic and impossible that the trees would ever come to the assault of the castle.

Nevertheless he decided to fortify his castle on the hill at Dunsinane, and for this purpose he ordered all his great nobility and thanes to send him stones and wood and other building materials, and to drag them with oxen up the steep hill to the castle.

Now among the nobles who were obliged to send oxen, horses, and materials to Dunsinane, was Macduff, Thane of Fife, a powerful lord, and both brave and wise. Macbeth suspected that he was a supporter of Malcolm and would go to his aid if ever he should come from England with an army, and hated him for it.

It happened that the King had summoned several of his nobles, including the Thane of Fife, to attend him at his castle of Dunsinane. They were all obliged to come, and none dared stay away, not even Macduff, who went to the King's Court as seldom as he could.

Now one day the King rode out with a few attendants to see the oxen drag the wood and the stones up the hill. They saw most of the oxen trudging up the hill with great difficulty. Their burdens were heavy, the weather was hot, and the hill was very steep.

Macbeth saw one pair of oxen so tired that they fell down under their load. The King was very angry and demanded to know who had sent oxen so weak and unfit for labour, when he had so much work for them to do.

" They belong to Macduff, the Thane of Fife," answered one of his attendants.

" Then," said the King in his great anger, " since the Thane of Fife sends such worthless cattle as these to do my labour, I will put his own neck into the yoke, and make him drag the burdens himself."

A friend of Macduff's, who was with the King, left him without being observed, and with all speed went to seek Macduff. He found him walking in the hall of the King's castle, while dinner was preparing. The instant Macduff heard what the

King had said, he knew that he had not a moment to lose.

Bidding a hasty farewell to his friend, he snatched up a loaf of bread from the table, called for his horses and servants, and was galloping back to his own province of Fife, before Macbeth had returned to the castle.

Macduff fled as fast as horses' feet could carry him ; but he was so ill provided with money for his expenses, that when he came to the great ferry over the river Tay, he had nothing to give the boatman who took them across except the loaf of bread he had snatched from the King's table. This ferry was for a long time afterwards called the Ferry of the Loaf.

Macduff reached his castle of Kennoway on the coast of Fife. He ordered his wife to shut the gates of the castle, draw up the drawbridge, and on no account to permit the King or any of his followers to enter. In the meantime, he went to the small harbour belonging to the castle and ordered a ship which was lying there to be fitted out for sea with all speed. Then bidding his wife farewell, he went on board, in order to escape from Macbeth.

The King and his guards were not far behind Macduff, and they were at the castle gates before Macduff had left. He called upon Lady Macduff to surrender the castle and to deliver up her husband. But Lady Macduff, who was a wise and a brave woman, made many excuses and delays, until she knew that the boat carrying her husband was safely out of the harbour.

Then mounting the wall of the castle she spoke boldly to the King.

" Do you see yon white sail upon the sea ? " she said. " Yonder goes Macduff to the Court of England. You will never see him again, till he comes back once more with young Prince Malcolm to pull you down from the throne, and to put you to death. You will never be able to put your yoke on the neck of Macduff, the Thane of Fife."

Macduff arrived at the Court of King Edward the Confessor, and joined Prince Malcolm, the son of Duncan. Macduff assured the King that the Scots were tired of the cruel Macbeth, and would join Prince Malcolm if he were to return to the country. King Edward thereupon ordered a great warrior, Siward, Earl of Northumberland, to lead a great army into Scotland to help Prince Malcolm recover his father's crown.

Then it happened just as Macduff had said. The Scottish thanes and nobles would not fight for Macbeth, but joined Prince Malcolm and Macduff against him. At length Macbeth shut himself up in his castle of Dunsinane, where he thought himself safe as he remembered the old women's prophecies.

By this time Malcolm and Macduff had come

as far as Birnam Wood, and lay encamped there with their army. The next morning they set off for Dunsinane, and every man, at Macduff's order, carried a bough of a tree, so that the enemy should not see how many men were coming against them.

News had reached Macbeth that the enemy were encamped at Birnam Wood, but still he thought himself safe. And then the sentinel who stood on the castle wall looked out towards Birnam Wood and saw the forest moving in the direction of the castle.

He ran to the King, who at first reviled him and threatened to put him to death. But the man entreated him to go to the wall himself, and so he mounted to the castle wall, and looking out, he knew the hour of his destruction had come.

His former bravery returned to him, and at the head of the few followers who remained faithful to him, he sallied out. He was killed, after a furious resistance, fighting hand to hand with Macduff in the thick of the battle.

Prince Malcolm mounted the throne, and his reign was long and prosperous. He rewarded Macduff by declaring that his descendants should always lead the vanguard of the Scottish army in battle, and to them also should be the honour of placing the crown on the King's head at the coronation.

THE STORY OF WILLIAM WALLACE

ONE day when William Wallace was a boy he went fishing for trout in the river of Irvine, near Ayr. He had caught a good many fish and was thinking of making for home, when two or three English soldiers, who belonged to the garrison of Ayr, came along and with their usual insolence ordered the boy to hand over the fish.

" Not all of them," said young Wallace; " they've taken me many hours to catch, and I must take a few home with me."

" Hand them over, you young puppy," cried one of the soldiers, coming a step nearer.

" No, I will not," cried Wallace, a determined look in his eyes.

" Oh, you won't; we shall see about that," said the man, striding towards the basket in which the fish lay. Wallace had no weapon, but he was still holding his fishing-rod, and before the man could reach the basket, he raised the rod and struck him so hard beneath the ear that he fell to the ground dead. Seizing the man's sword he fought with so much fury that he put the other men to flight. He then hastened home with all speed, for he had not a moment to lose.

He knew that the soldier's death would be reported to the English governor of Ayr, and that the governor would issue orders for his arrest. And indeed he was right ; the soldiers sought long for him, but he lay concealed among the hills and woods of the country until they tired of their search and the matter was forgotten.

His hatred for the English who ruled his country with so much violence and tyranny grew more intense, and in the years that followed he had many other adventures of the same kind. Sometimes when alone, sometimes with a few companions, he gallantly defended himself against superior numbers of the English, until his name became a terror to them.

The English at that time, under King Edward I, had reduced Scotland almost entirely to the condition of a conquered country. English soldiers had been placed in garrisons in different castles of Scotland. They thought themselves masters of the country and treated the Scots with great contempt. They took whatever they had a fancy to, and treated with cruelty and violence any Scot who refused their slightest wish.

Feeling was strong against the English, and the people whispered amongst themselves that if only they had a great leader to command them, they would rise up in a body and recover the liberty and independence of their country.

Such a leader arose in William Wallace. He was tall and handsome and one of the strongest and bravest men that ever lived. His skill in the use of weapons was known throughout the land, and his latest exploits against the English were on every lip.

Rumours and legends grew up around his name, and it is a great pity that we do not know the exact details of many of his exploits. We do know, however, the action which was the cause of his final rising in arms.

Wallace was living quietly with his wife in the town of Lanark, and one day, as he walked in the market-place, dressed in a green garment, with a rich dagger by his side, an Englishman came up and insulted him. He said that no Scotsman had any business to wear so gay a costume, or carry so handsome a weapon. It soon came to a quarrel, as on many former occasions ; and Wallace, having killed the Englishman, fled to his own house. English soldiers speedily assaulted the house, and while they were endeavouring to force their way in at the front of the house, Wallace escaped by a back door. He fled to a rugged and rocky glen, near Lanark, all covered with bushes and trees and full of high precipices, where he knew he would be safe from the English soldiers.

In the meantime, the governor of Lanark burned Wallace's house, and put his wife and servants to death. He proclaimed Wallace an outlaw, and offered a reward to anyone who should bring him to an English garrison, alive or dead.

The cruel actions of the governor raised to the highest pitch the hatred which Wallace had always borne against the English. He soon collected a body of men—men outlawed like himself or willing to become so rather than endure the oppression of the English any longer.

One of his earliest expeditions was against the governor of Lanark, whom he killed, and thus avenged the death of his wife. He fought skirmishes against the soldiers who were sent against him, and often defeated them, and as the news of his successes spread, multitudes joined his standard, until at length he was at the head of a considerable army.

News reached Wallace of the murder of his uncle, Sir Reginald Crawford, Sheriff of the County of Ayr, at the hands of the English. It appeared that the English governor of Ayr had invited the greater part of the Scottish nobility in the western parts of Scotland to meet him at some large buildings called the Barns of Ayr, for the purpose of friendly conference about the affairs of the nation—or so he said.

Actually he had planned a treacherous means of putting the Scottish nobles to death. The English soldiers prepared a number of halters with running nooses, and hung them from the beams which supported the roof. And then as the Scottish nobles were admitted two at a time, the nooses were thrown over their heads, and they were pulled up by the neck and thus hanged or strangled to death. Among those who were slain in this base and treacherous manner was Wallace's uncle.

Wallace was resolved to be revenged on the authors of this great crime, and with his followers hastened towards Ayr. They halted in a wood near the town, and news reached him that the English kept no guard or watch in the town, not suspecting that there were any enemies so near them. After the English had eaten and drunken plentifully, they lay down to sleep in the same large barns in which they had murdered the noblemen, and when Wallace arrived they were sleeping heavily.

Wallace directed a woman who knew the place to mark with chalk the doors of the buildings where the English lay. Then he sent a party of men, who with strong ropes made all the doors so fast on the outside that those within could not open them. On the outside the Scots had prepared heaps of straw, to which they set fire, and the barns being made of wood, were soon burning in a bright flame. The English were awakened and endeavoured to get out to save their lives, but it was in vain, and great numbers perished miserably.

Not long afterwards messengers arrived bearing

news that a great English army, led by John de Warenne, Earl of Surrey, was approaching. Wallace was not dismayed : his party grew daily stronger, and more and more Scottish nobles were joining him, although some of them left when they heard the news of the English army.

He had taken up his camp upon the northern side of the river Forth, near the town of Stirling, where the river was crossed by a long wooden bridge. The English general approached the banks of the river on the southern side, and sent two clergymen to offer a pardon to Wallace and his followers if they would lay down their arms.

" Go back to Warenne," said Wallace, " and tell him we value not the pardon of the King of England. We are not here for the purpose of treating for peace, but of abiding battle and restoring freedom to our country. Let the English come on —we defy them to their very beards."

This proud reply infuriated the English leaders, and they pressed forward for battle. Against the advice of one or two experienced soldiers the English army began to cross the narrow wooden bridge at Stirling. Wallace allowed a considerable part of the English army to pass the bridge without offering opposition, but when about a half of the men were over, and the bridge was crowded with those who were following, he charged those who had crossed with his whole strength. He slew a very great number, and drove the rest into the river Forth, where the greater part were drowned. The remainder of the English army who were left on the southern bank fled in confusion, having first set fire to the wooden bridge, that the Scots should not pursue them.

The Scots, however, quickly crossed the river and attacked the castles in which the English soldiers were sheltering, and took most of them by force or by stratagem. Wallace's army chased the remnants of the English almost entirely out of Scotland, regained the towns and castles of which they had possessed themselves, and recovered for a time the complete freedom of the country.

Edward I was in Flanders when these events took place, and when he heard that Scotland, which he thought completely subdued, had risen in a great rebellion against him, defeated his armies, chased his soldiers out of the country, and invaded England with a great force, he hastened home. He came back from Flanders in a mighty rage, and determined not to leave the rebellious country until it was finally conquered, for which purpose he assembled a very fine army and marched into Scotland.

In the meantime the Scots prepared to defend themselves, and chose Wallace to be Governor or Protector of the kingdom, as they had no king at the time. But although Wallace was the best soldier and the bravest man in Scotland, and therefore the most fitted to be in command at this critical time, many Scottish nobles were envious of him, because he was not a man born in high rank or enjoying a large estate. His father was indeed only a private gentleman, of Ellerslie in Renfrewshire. So great was the jealousy of some of the nobles that they said that they would not have a man of inferior position to be general over them, and that they would refuse to fight with him against the English.

However, the lower classes were greatly attached to Wallace, and with their support he assembled a large army. He marched boldly against the King of England, and met him near the town of Falkirk. Most of the Scottish army were on foot, for in those days only the nobility and great men of Scotland fought on horseback. The English, on the other hand, had a very large body of the finest cavalry in the world, Normans and English, all clothed in complete armour. King Edward also had the celebrated archers of England, each of whom was said to carry twelve Scotsmen's lives under his girdle, because every archer had twelve arrows stuck in his belt and was expected to kill a man with every arrow.

The Scots had some good archers from the Forest of Ettrick, but they were not nearly equal in number to the English. The greater part of the

Scottish army were armed with long spears. They were placed thick and close together, and laid all their spears so close, point over point, that it seemed as difficult to break through them as through the wall of a strong castle.

The battle was long and fierce. The English cavalry charged the Scottish ranks again and again, and each time they failed to break the solid ranks of the Scottish footmen with their long spears. The Scots stood their ground, and many of the English horses were thrown to the ground, and the riders were killed as the horses lay rolling, unable to rise owing to the weight of their heavy armour.

When King Edward saw that his cavalry were repeatedly beaten off with heavy losses and failed to break the wood of spears, he commanded his archers to advance. They approached within arrow-shot of the Scottish ranks, and poured on them such close and dreadful volleys of arrows that it was impossible for the gallant Scots to hold out. The English cavalry charged again and broke through the ranks, which were by then in disorder.

William Wallace was not captured, but after this fatal defeat he resigned his office of Governor of Scotland. He refused, however, either to acknowledge the usurper Edward, or to lay down his arms, and with a small band of followers he continued to live among the woods and mountains of his native country. A great reward was set upon his head, and many attempts and traps were set to catch him, but for no less than seven years he remained free.

At length he was betrayed—it is said by a Scotsman, Sir John Menteith by name—and he was brought to London to stand his trial in Westminster Hall before the English judges. He was accused of having been a traitor to the English Crown, to which he answered :

" I could not be a traitor to Edward, for I never was his subject."

He was charged with many crimes, and he replied to the charges with calm resolution : " It is true I have killed many Englishmen, but it was because they had come to subdue and oppress my native country. I do not repent what I have done, I am only sorry that I did not put many more of them to death."

Notwithstanding that Wallace's defence was a good one, both in law and common sense—for surely every one has not only a right to fight in defence of his native country but is bound in duty to do so—the English judges condemned him to death.

And so Sir William Wallace, one of the greatest patriots in the cause of Scottish liberty, and whose name is ever remembered in every Scottish home, was executed in London.

SPEARS AND JACKS

AMONG the lords in most constant attendance upon King James III of Scotland was Lord Somerville, a nobleman who had a reputation for most generous hospitality.

It was his custom when he intended to return to his castle with a party of guests to send on a man ahead with a message on which were written the words " Speates and raxes " ; these are the Latin words, for " spits " and " ranges," by which hint he meant that a great quantity of food should be prepared, and that the spits and ranges, or framework on which they turn, should be put into action.

Lord Somerville's reputation for hospitality reached the ears of the King, and he expressed a wish to visit him at his castle of Cowthally, near the town of Carnwath. Lord Somerville immediately sent off a special messenger ; but even the visit of the King himself did not induce him to change his usual manner of announcing his return, except that he repeated the phrase three times, thinking no doubt that a considerable retinue would accompany the King, and that consequently more food than usual would be required.

The paper was delivered to Lady Somerville,

who, having been only recently married, was not quite accustomed to read her husband's handwriting, which probably was not very good, for in the fifteenth century noblemen used the sword more than the pen.

So the lady sent for the steward, and after laying their heads together, instead of reading " Speates and raxes," they made out the writing to be " Spears and jacks." Jacks were a sort of leather doublet covered with plates of iron, which were worn as armour by horsemen of inferior rank.

Lady Somerville concluded the meaning of these terrible words to be that her Lord was in some distress, or engaged in some quarrel in Edinburgh, and needed assistance, so that instead of collecting cattle and preparing for a feast, they collected armed men together and got ready for a fray. A party of two hundred horsemen was speedily assembled, and they were trotting over the moors towards Edinburgh, when they observed a large company of gentlemen hawking on the side of a hill.

It was the King and Lord Somerville, who were on their way to Cowthally, taking their sport as they went. When the King saw Lord Somerville's banner at the head of the troop, he concluded that it was some rebellious enterprise, and charged the Baron with treason.

Lord   Somerville   declared   his   innocence.

" Yonder," said he, " are indeed my men and my banner, but I have no knowledge whatever of the cause that has brought them here. If your Grace will permit me to ride forward I will soon see the reason of this disturbance. Let my eldest son and heir remain as a hostage in your Grace's power, and let him lose his head if I prove false to my duty."

Lord Somerville rode towards his followers and the matter was easily explained. The mistake was then only a subject of merriment, and the King, looking at the letter, protested that he himself would have read " Spears and jacks."

And so they moved on to Cowthally. Lady Somerville was much out of countenance at the mistake, but the King praised her for the speed with which she had raised the men to assist her husband and step-son, and said he hoped she would always have as brave a band at his service when the King and Kingdom required them. And thus everything went off happily.

BRUCE AND THE SPIDER

R OBERT THE BRUCE fought with William Wallace in the wars against the English, and for bravery and strength of arm he was almost his master's equal. His courage, too, was as great except on the fatal day of the battle of Falkirk, when Wallace was defeated and fled to the mountains. After the battle Bruce's courage failed him ; he feared that they would never recover the freedom of Scotland, and fearing too that the victorious English King would confiscate his estates, he submitted to King Edward I.

For a time he even bore arms with the English against such bands of his countrymen who still continued to resist the English King. But at length his courage returned, and he realised that every blow he struck for the English King was another blow against his brave countrymen who were fighting for the independence of Scotland.

And so he left the English army and began to gather round him a gallant force of men, many of them drawn from the most noble families of the land. Wallace was dead, and Bruce was held to be the best warrior in all Scotland. He was wise and prudent, and an excellent general, and men flocked to join him. He was generous too, and courteous by nature, but he had some faults, which perhaps belonged as much to the fierce period in which he lived as to his own character. He was rash and passionate, and in his passion he was sometimes relentless and cruel. Many of his misfortunes were due to his rashness and cruelty, and none more so than in his quarrel with John Comyn, a powerful Scottish nobleman.

John Comyn, or Red Comyn as he is usually called, and Robert Bruce were at this time the two principal candidates for the Crown of Scotland. Bruce went to see Comyn, it is said, to enlist his help in driving out the English, but they quarrelled and fought, and Bruce killed Red Comyn. This was indeed a rash and foolish act, and the memory of it haunted Bruce for the rest of his life.

After the deed was done he realised that he must act now or not at all. He drew his own followers together, and summoned to meet him the barons who were still willing to support him. He was then crowned King, with a small circlet of gold which had been hurriedly made to represent the ancient crown of Scotland which Edward I had carried away to England.

The news reached the English King of this new attempt to shake off his authority, and immediately he set off at the head of a large army to march against Bruce. Bruce was defeated, and escaped with only a few followers into the mountains of the Highlands.

They were driven from one place in the Highlands to another, starved out in some districts, and forced from others by the opposition of the inhabitants. Bruce found enemies everywhere. Time and time again he was attacked by the English and by Scottish chiefs, who were friendly to the English, and because of their superior numbers he was almost always defeated. But in spite of these defeats he remained undaunted, and kept up his own spirits and those of his followers.

At one time, however, such great misfortunes befell him that he almost gave up his fight to regain the freedom of Scotland. News reached him that his wife, who had been left for safety in the castle of Kildrummie, had been captured by the English, and his youngest brother, Nigel Bruce, who had been left to defend the castle, had been killed.

Bruce and his handful of followers were spending the winter on the bare island of Rachrin, off the coast of Ireland, and one morning, soon after this unhappy news reached him, he was lying on his bed turning over in his mind the events of the past months. What should he do now ? Should he give up all idea of driving out the English, dismiss his followers, and with his brothers go to the Holy Land to fight against the Saracens ? On the other hand however, he thought, it would be both criminal and cowardly to give up while the slightest chance of success remained.

While he was thus reflecting, Bruce looked upward to the roof of the cabin where he lay, and his eye was attracted by a spider.

The spider was hanging at the end of a long thread of its own spinning, and was endeavouring to swing itself from one beam in the roof to another, for the purpose of fixing the line on which it meant to stretch its web.

The spider made the attempt again and again without success, and Bruce watched it make the attempt no less than six times. Six times—it came into his head that he had himself fought just six battles against the English and their allies, and that the spider was in the same position as himself. They had both tried six times and they had both failed.

" Now," thought Bruce, " I will be guided by the luck of the spider, and if the insect makes another effort to fix its thread and is successful, then I will venture a seventh time to try my fortune in Scotland. But if the spider fails, I will go to the Holy Land, and never more return to my native country."

He watched the spider as he made this resolution. The spider gathered all its strength, and swinging towards the beam that had eluded it so often, succeeded in fastening its thread.

Bruce, seeing the success of the spider, resolved

to try again ; and whether this story is true—and there is indeed no reason to doubt it is not—Bruce, who had never before gained a victory, was never afterwards utterly defeated. And it is said that people of the name of Bruce are so completely persuaded of the truth of this story that they will on no account kill a spider, because it was that insect which had shown the example of perseverance, and given a signal of good luck to their great namesake.

THE GOODMAN OF BALLENGIECH

LIKE his father, King James V had a custom of going about the country disguised as an ordinary man, in order that he might hear complaints which might not otherwise reach his ears.

Many stories are told of what befell him upon such journeys. On one occasion, King James, being alone and in disguise, fell into a quarrel with some gypsies, and was assaulted by four or five of them. This chanced to be very near the bridge of Cramond, so the King got on the bridge, which, as it was high and narrow, enabled him to defend himself with his sword against the men by whom he was attacked.

There was a poor man threshing corn in a barn nearby, who came out on hearing the noise of the scuffle, and seeing one man defending himself against so many, gallantly took the King's part with his flail, to such good purpose that the gypsies were obliged to fly.

The husbandman then took the King into the barn, brought him a towel and water to wash the blood from his face and hands, and finally walked with him a little way towards Edinburgh, in case he should again be attacked.

On the way the King asked his companion what

and who he was. The labourer answered that his name was John Howieson, and that he was a bondsman on the farm of Braehead, near Cramond, which belonged to the King of Scotland.

James then asked the poor man if there was any wish in the world which he would particularly desire should be fulfilled ; and honest John confessed he would think himself the happiest man in Scotland were he but proprietor of the farm on which he worked as a labourer.

He then asked the King, in turn, who *he* was ; and James replied, as usual, that he was the Goodman of Ballengiech, a poor man who had a small appointment about the palace ; but he added that if John Howieson would come to see him on the next Sunday, he would endeavour to repay his manful assistance, and at least give him the pleasure of seeing the royal apartments.

John put on his best clothes, and appearing at a postern-gate of the palace, inquired for the Goodman of Ballengiech. The King had given orders that he should be admitted ; and John found his friend, the goodman, in the same disguise which he had worn before. The King, still preserving the character of a minor official of the household, conducted John Howieson from one apartment of the palace to another, and was amused with his wonder and his remarks.

At length James asked his visitor if he would like

to see the King ; to which John replied, nothing would delight him so much, if he could do so without giving offence.

The Goodman of Ballengiech, of course, undertook that the King would not be angry, " But," said John, " how am I to know his Grace from the nobles who will be all about him ? "

" Easily," replied his companion ; " all the others will be uncovered—the King alone will wear his hat or bonnet."

So speaking, King James introduced the countryman into a great hall, which was filled by the nobility and officers of the Crown. John was a little frightened, and drew close to his attendant ; but was still unable to distinguish the King.

" I told you that you should know him by his wearing his hat," said the conductor.

" Then," said John, after he had again looked round the room, " it must be either you or me, for all but us two are bare-headed."

The King laughed at John's fancy ; and that the good yeoman might have occasion for mirth also, he made him a present of the farm of Braehead, which he had wished so much to possess, on condition that John Howieson, or his successors, should be ready to present a ewer and basin for the King to wash his hands, when his Majesty should come to Holyrood Palace or should pass the bridge of Cramond.

Nearly three hundred years later, a descendant of John Howieson of Braehead still possessed the estate which was given to his ancestor, and when George IV came to Scotland in 1822, he offered his Majesty water from a silver ewer that he might perform the service by which he held his lands.

KINMONT WILLIE

I WELL remember the dull April morning, in the year 1596, when my father, William Armstrong of Kinmont—" Kinmont Willie," as he was called by all the countryside—set out with me for a ride into Cumberland.

As a rule, when he set his face that way, he rode armed, and with all his men behind him, for these were the old reiving days, when we folk who dwelt on the Scottish side of the Border thought we had a right to go and steal what we could, sheep or oxen, or even hay, from the English loons, who, in their turn, would come slipping over from their side to take liberties with us, and mayhap burn down a house or two in the by-going.

Well, as I say, my father was not riding on business, as it were, this morning, for just then there was a truce for a day or two between the countries, the two Wardens of the Marches, Sir Walter Scott of Buccleuch and My Lord Scroope, having sent their deputies to meet and settle some affairs at the Dayholme of Kershope, where a burn divides England from Scotland. My father and I had attended the Truce Muster, and were riding homeward with but a handful of men, when I took a sudden notion into my head that I would like to cross the Border, and ride a few miles on English ground.

My birthday had fallen the week before (I was just eleven years old), and my father, aye kind to his motherless bairns, had given me a new pony, a little shaggy beast from Galloway, and, as I was keen to see how it would run beside a big man's horse, I had pled hard for permission to accompany him on it to the Muster.

As a rule I never rode with him. " I was too young for the work," he would say ; but that day he gave his consent, only making the bargain that there should be no crying out or grumbling if I were tired or hungry long ere we got home again.

The Truce Muster had broken up sooner than he expected, so my father saw no reason why he should not grant my request and let me have a canter on English soil, for on a day of truce we could cross the Border if we chose without the risk of being taken prisoners by Lord Scroope's men, and marched off to Carlisle Castle, while the English had a like privilege, and could ride down Liddesdale in open daylight, if they were so minded.

Scarce had we crossed the little burn, however, which runs between low-growing hazel bushes, and separates us from England, when two of the men rode right into a bog, and when, after some half-

"MY FATHER EYED THEM KEENLY, HIS FACE GROWING GRAVE AS HE DID SO"

hour's work, we got the horses out again, we found that both of them wanted a shoe, and my father said at once that we must go straight home, in case they went lame.

At this I drew a long face. I had never been into England, and it was a sore disappointment to be turned back just when we had reached it.

"Well, well," said my father, laughing, ever soft-hearted where I was concerned, "I suppose I must e'en take thee a ride into Bewcastle, lad, since we have got this length. The men can go back with the horses ; 'tis safe enough to go alone to-day."

So the men turned back, and my father and I rode on for eight miles or so, over that most desolate country.

"Hast had enough ? " said my father at last. "If summer were once and here, I'll let thee ride with the troop, and mayhap thou wilt get a glimpse of ' Merrie Carlisle,' as they call it. It lies over there, twelve miles or more from where we stand."

As he pointed out the direction with his whip, we both became aware of a large body of men riding rapidly over the moor as if to meet us. My father eyed them keenly, his face growing grave as he did so. "Who are they, father ? " I asked with a sinking heart.

"It's Sakelde, the English Warden's deputy, and no friend o' mine," he answered with a frown,

" and on any other day I would not have met him alone like this for a hundred merks ; but the truce holds for three days yet, so we are quite safe ; all the same, lad, we had better turn our horses round, and slip in behind that little hill ; they may not have noticed us, and in that case 'tis no use rousing their curiosity."

Alas ! we had no sooner set our horses to the trot, than it became apparent that not only were we observed, but that for some reason or other the leader of the band of horsemen was desirous of barring our way.

He gave an order—we could see him pointing with his hand—and at once his men spurred on their horses and began to spread out so as to surround us. Then my father swore a big oath, and plunged his spurs into his horse's sides. " Come on, Jock," he shouted, " sit tight and be a man ; if we can only get over the hill edge at Kershope, they'll pay for this yet."

I will remember that race to my dying day. It appeared to last for hours, but it could not have lasted many minutes, ten at the most, during which time all the blood in my body seemed to be pounding and surging in my head, and the green grass and the sky to be flying past me, all mixed up together, and behind, and on all sides, came the pit-pat of horses' feet, and then someone seized my pony's rein, and brought him up with a jerk, and

my father and I were sitting in the midst of two
hundred armed riders, whose leader, a tall man,
with a thin cunning face, regarded us with a
triumphant smile.

"Neatly caught, thou thieving rogue," he said;
"by my troth, neatly caught. Who would have
thought that Kinmont Willie would have been
such a fool as to venture so far from home without
an escort? But I can supply the want, and thou
shalt ride to Carlisle right well attended, and shall
never now lack a guard till thou partest with thy
life at Haribee."

As the last word fell on my ear, I turned sick
and faint, and all the crowd of men and horses
seemed to whirl round and round. Haribee!
Right well I knew that fateful name, for it was the
place at Carlisle where they hanged prisoners.

"'Tis a day of truce," I gasped with dry lips;
but the men around me only laughed, and I could
hear that my father's fierce remonstrance met with
no better answer.

"Thou art well named, thou false Sakelde," I
heard him say, and his voice shook with fury, "for
no man of honour would break the King's truce in
this way."

But Sakelde only gave orders to his men to bind
their prisoner, saying, as he did so, "I warrant
Lord Scroope will be too glad to see thee to think
much about the truce, and if thou art so scrupu-

lous, thou needest not be hanged for a couple of days ; the walls of Carlisle Castle are thick enough to guard thee till then. Be quick, my lads," he went on, turning to his men ; " we have a good fourteen miles to ride yet, and I have no mind to be benighted ere we reach firmer ground."

So they tied my father's feet together under his horse, and his hands behind his back, and fastened his bridle rein to that of a trooper, and the word was given for the men to form up.

I followed in the rear with a heavy heart. I could easily have escaped had I wanted to do so, for no one paid any attention to me ; but I felt that, as long as I could, I must stay near my father.

The spring evening was fast drawing to a close as we came to the banks of the Liddle. As we paused at a ford for a moment or two to give the horses a drink, my father's voice rang out above the careless jesting of the troopers.

" Let me say good-bye to my eldest son, Sakelde, and send him home ; or do the English war with bairns ? "

I saw the blood rise to the English leader's thin sallow face at the taunt, but he answered quietly enough, " Let the boy speak to him and then go back," and a way was opened up for me to where my father sat, a bound and helpless prisoner, on his huge white horse.

One trooper, kinder than the rest, took my

pony's rein as I slid off its back and ran to him. Many a time when I was little, had I had a ride on White Charlie, and I needed no help to scramble up to my old place on the big horse's neck.

My father could not move, but he looked down at me with all the anger and defiance gone out of his face, and a look on it which I had only seen there once before, and that was when he lifted me up on his knee after my mother died and told me that I must do my best to help him, and try to look after the little ones.

That look upset me altogether, and, forgetting the many eyes that watched us, and the fact that I was eleven years old and almost a man, I threw my arms round his neck and kissed him again and again, sobbing and greeting as any bairn might have done.

" Ride home, laddie, and God be with ye. Remember if I fall that thou art the head of the house, and see that thou do honour to the name," he said aloud. Then he signed to me to go, and, just as I was clambering down, resting a toe in his stirrup, he made a tremendous effort and bent down over me. " If thou could'st but get word to the Lord of Buccleuch, laddie, 'tis my only chance. They dare not touch me for two days yet. Tell him I was ta'en by treachery at the time o' truce."

The whisper was so low I could hardly hear it,

and yet in a moment I understood all it was meant to convey, and my heart beat until I thought that the whole of Sakelde's troopers must read my secret in my face as I passed through them to where my pony stood.

With a word of thanks I took the rein from the kindly man who had held it, and then stood watching the body of riders as they splashed through the ford and disappeared in the twilight, leaving me alone.

But I felt there was work for me to do, and a ray of hope stole into my heart. True, it was more than twenty miles, as the crow flies, to Branksome Tower in Teviotdale, where my Lord of Buccleuch lived, and I did not know the road, which lay over some of the wildest hills of the Border country, but I knew that he was a great man, holding King James' commission as Warden of the Scottish Marches, and at his bidding the whole countryside would rise to a man—'twas well known that he bore no love to the English. I knew that it was no use going home to Kinmont for a man to ride with me, for it was out of my way, and would only be a waste of time.

It was almost dark now, but I knew that the moon would rise in three or four hours, and then there would be light enough for me to try to thread my way over the hills that lay between the valleys of the Teviot and Liddle. In the meantime, there was no special need to hurry, so I loosened my pony's rein and let him nibble away at the short sweet grass which was just beginning to spring, while I unbuckled the bag of cakes which I had put up so gaily in the morning, and, taking one out, along with a bit of cheese, did my best to make a hearty meal. But I was not very successful, for when the heart is heavy, food goes down but slowly.

Although I had been down the Liddle as far as the ford once or twice before, it had always been in daylight, and my father had been with me ; but I knew that as long as I kept close to the river I was all right for the first few miles, until the valley narrowed in, and then I must strike off among the high hills on my left.

It was slow work, for it was too dark to ride, and I dare not leave the water in case I lost my way.

At last, just when the tears were getting very near my eyes—for I was but a little chap to be set on such a desperate errand—I struck on a narrow road which led up a brae to my left, and going along it for a hundred yards or so, I saw a light which seemed to come from a cottage window.

In those lawless days one had to be cautious about going up to strange houses, for one never knew whether one would find a friend or an enemy within, so I determined to tie my pony to a tree, and steal noiselessly up to the building, and see what sort of place it was.

I did so, and found that the light came from a tiny thatched cottage standing by itself, sheltered by some fir trees. There appeared to be no dogs about, so I crept quite close to the little window, and peered in through a hole in the shutter. I could see the inside of the room quite plainly; it was poorly furnished, but beautifully clean. In a corner opposite the window stood a rough settle, while on a three-legged stool by the peat fire sat an old woman knitting busily, a collie dog at her feet.

There could be nothing to fear from her, so I knocked boldly at the door. The collie flew to the back of it barking furiously, but I heard the old woman calling him back, and presently she peeped out, asking who was there.

" 'Tis I, Jock Armstrong of Kinmont," I said, " and I fain would be guided as to the quickest road to Branksome Tower."

The old woman peered over my head into the darkness, evidently expecting to see someone standing behind me.

" I ken Willie o' Kinmont; but he's a grown man," she said suspiciously, making as though she would shut the door.

" He's my father," I cried, vainly endeavouring to keep my voice steady, " and—and—I have a message to carry from him to the Lord of Buccleuch at Branksome." I would fain have told the whole story, but I knew it was better to be cautious, for I was still no distance from the English Border.

"Loshsake, laddie!" exclaimed the old dame in astonishment, setting the door wide open so that the light might fall full on me, "'tis full twenty miles tae Branksome, an' it's a bad road ower the hills."

"But I have a pony," I said. "'Tis tied up down the roadway there, and the moon will rise."

"That it will in an hour or two, but all the same I misdoubt me that you'll lose your road. What's the matter wi' Kinmont Willie, that he has tae send a bairn like you his messages? Ye needna' be feared to speak out," she added as I hesitated; "Kinmont Willie is a friend of mine —at least, he did my goodman and me a good turn once—and I would like to pay it back again if I could."

I needed no second bidding. The old woman listened attentively to my story, and then shook her fist in the direction which the English had taken.

"He's a fause loon that Sakelde," she said, "and I'd walk to Carlisle any day to see him hanged. Keep up your heart, my man; if you can get to the Bold Buccleuch he'll put things right, I'll warrant, and I'll do all I can for you,

Go inbye, and sit down by the fire, and I'll go down the road and fetch the nag. You'll both be the better for a rest, and a bite o' something to eat, and when the moon is risen I'll take you up the hill, and show you the track. My goodman is away at Hawick market, or he would ha'e ridden a bit of the road wi' ye."

After Allison Elliot, for that was her name, had brought my pony into her cow-house, and seen that he was supplied with both hay and water, she returned to the cottage, and with her own hands took off my coarse woollen hose and heavy shoon, and spread them on the hearth to dry, then she made me lie down on the settle, and, covering me up with a plaid, she bade me go to sleep, promising to wake me the moment the moon rose.

It was nearly eleven o'clock when she shook me gently, saying it was time to be going, and, sitting up, I found a supper of wheaten bread and hot milk on the table, which she told me to eat, while she wrapped herself in a plaid and went out for the nag.

What with the sleep, and the dry clothes, and the warm food, I promise you I felt twice the man I had done a few hours earlier. The moon was only beginning to rise, and there was still but little light. After we had gone some two miles, we struck a bridle track which wound upwards between two high hills.

Here Allison paused and looked keenly at the ground.

" This is the path," she said ; " you can hardly lose it, for there have been riders over it yesterday or the day before. This will lead you over by Priesthaugh Swire, and down the Allan into Teviot-dale. Beware of a bog which you will pass some two miles on this side of Priesthaugh. May the Lord be good to you, laddie, and grant you a safe convoy, for ye carry a brave heart in that little body o' yours ! "

I thanked her with all my might, promising to go back and see her if my errand were successful ; then I turned my pony's head to the hills, and spurred him into a brisk canter. He was a willing little beast, and mightily refreshed by Allison Elliot's hay, and as the moon was now shining clearly, we made steady progress ; but it was a long lonely ride for a boy of my age, and once or twice my courage nearly failed me : once when my pony put his foot into a sheep drain, and stumbled, throwing me clean over his head, and again when I missed the track, and rode straight into the bog Allison had warned me about, and in which the little beast was near sticking altogether, and I lost a good hour getting him to firm land and finding the track again.

The bright morning sun was showing above the eastern horizon before I left the weary hills behind me, but it was easy work to ride down the sloping banks of the Allan, and soon I came to the wooded valley of the Teviot.

Urging on my tired pony, I cantered down the level haughs which lay by the riverside, and it was not long before Branksome came in sight, a high square house, with many rows of windows, flanked by a massive square tower at each corner.

I rode up to the great doorway through an avenue of beeches and knocked timidly on the wrought-iron knocker.

The old seneschal who came to the door looked me up and down with a broad grin on his face before he asked who I was, and on what business I had come.

"To see my Lord of Buccleuch, and carry a message to him from William Armstrong of Kinmont," I replied, with as much dignity as I could muster, for the fellow's smile angered me, and I feared that he might not think it worth his while to tell the Warden of my arrival.

"Then thou shalt see Sir Walter at once, young sir, if thou wilt walk this way," said the man, mimicking my voice good-naturedly, and hitching my pony's bridle to an iron ring in the door-post, he led me along a stone passage, straight into a great vaulted hall, in the centre of which stood a long wooden table, with a smaller one standing crossways on a dais at its head.

A crowd of squires and men-at-arms stood round the lower table, laughing and jesting as they helped themselves with their hunting knives to slices from the huge joints, or quaffed great tankards of ale, while up at the top sat my Lord of Buccleuch himself, surrounded by his knights, and waited on by smart pages in livery, boys about my own age.

As the old seneschal appeared in the doorway there was a sudden silence, while he announced in a loud voice that a messenger had arrived from William Armstrong of Kinmont ; but when he stepped aside, and everyone saw that the messenger was only a little eleven-years-old lad, a loud laugh went round the hall, and the smart pages whispered together and pointed to my muddy clothes.

When the old seneschal saw this, he gave me a kindly nudge.

"Yonder is my Lord of Buccleuch at the top of the table," he whispered ; "go right up to him, and speak out thy message boldly."

I did as I was bid, though I felt my cheeks burn as I walked up the great hall, among staring men and whispering pages, and when I reached the dais where the Warden sat, I knelt at his feet, cap in hand, as my father had taught me to do before my betters.

Sir Walter Scott, Lord of Buccleuch, of whom

I had heard so much, was a young, stern-looking man, with curly brown hair and keen blue eyes. His word was law on the Borders, and people said that even the King, in far-off Edinburgh, stood in awe of him ; but he leant forward and spoke kindly enough to me.

" So thou comest from Armstrong of Kinmont, boy ; and had Kinmont Willie no better messenger at hand, that he had to fall back on a smatchet like thee ? "

" There were plenty of men at Kinmont, an' it please your lordship," I answered, " had I had time to seek them ; but a man called Sakelde hath ta'en my father prisoner, and carried him to Carlisle, and I have ridden all night to tell thee of it, for he is like to be hanged the day after to-morrow, if thou canst not save him."

Here my voice gave way, and I could only cling to the great man's knee, for my quivering lips refused to say any more.

Buccleuch put his arm round me, and spoke slowly, as one would speak to a bairn.

" And who is thy father, little man ? "

" Kinmont Willie," I gasped, " and he was ta'en last night, in truce time."

I felt the arm that was round me stiffen, and there was silence for a moment, then my lord swore a great oath, and let his clenched fist fall so heavily on the table, that the red French wine which stood before him splashed right out of the beaker, a foot or two in the air.

"My Lord of Scroope shall answer for this," he cried. "Hath he forgotten that men name me the Bold Buccleuch, and that I am Keeper o' the Scottish Marches, to see that justice is done to high and low, gentle and simple?"

Then he gave some quick, sharp orders, and ten or twelve men left the room, and a minute later I saw them, through a casement, throw themselves astride their horses, and gallop out of the courtyard. At the sight my heart lightened, for I knew that whatever could be done for my father would be done, for these men had gone to "warn the waters," or, in other words, to carry the tidings far and wide, and bid all the men of the Western Border be ready to meet their chief at some given trysting-place, and ride with him to the rescue.

Meanwhile, the Warden lifted me on his knee, and began asking me questions, while the pages gathered round, no longer jeering, but with wide-open eyes.

"Thou art a brave lad," he said at last, after I had told him the whole story, "and, with thy father's permission, I would fain have thee for one of my pages."

At any other time my heart would have leapt at this unheard-of good fortune, for to be a page in the Warden's household was the ambition of every well-born lad on the Border ; but at that moment I felt as if Buccleuch hardly realised my father's danger.

"But he is lodged in Carlisle Castle, and men say the walls are thick," I said anxiously, "and it is garrisoned by my Lord Scroope's soldiers."

The Warden laughed.

"We will teach my Lord Scroope that there is no bird's nest that the Bold Buccleuch dare not harry," he said, and, seeing the look on his face, I was content.

Then, noticing how weary I was, he called one of the older pages, and bade him see that I had food and rest, and the boy, who had been one of the first to laugh before, but who now treated me with respect, took me away to a little turret room which he shared with some of his fellows, and brought me a piece of venison pie, and then left me to go to sleep on his low pallet, promising to wake me when there were signs of the Warden and his men setting out.

I must have slept the whole day, for the little room was almost dark again, and the rain was beating wildly on the casement, when the boy came back. "My lord hath given orders for the horses to be saddled," he said, "and the trysting-place is Woodhouselee."

It did not take me long to spring up and fasten my doublet, and follow my guide down to the great hall. Here all was bustle and confusion, while outside in the courtyard some fifty or sixty horses were standing, ready saddled, with bags of fodder thrown over their necks.

Every few minutes a handful of men would ride up in the dusk, and, leaving their rough mountain ponies outside, would stride into the hall, and begin to eat as hard as they could, exchanging greetings between the mouthfuls. These were men from the neighbourhood, my friend informed me, mostly kinsmen of Buccleuch, and lairds in their own right, who had ridden to Branksome with their men to start with their chief.

There was Scott of Harden, and Scott of Goldilands, Scott of Commonside, and Scott of Allanhaugh, and many more whom I do not now remember, and they drank their ale, and laughed and joked, as if they were riding to a wedding, instead of on an errand which might cost them their lives.

Buccleuch himself was in the midst of them, booted and spurred, and presently his eye fell on me.

"Ha! my young cocksparrow," he cried. "Wilt ride with us to greet thy father, or are thy bones too weary? Small shame 'twould be to thee if they were."

"Oh, if it please thee, sire, let me ride," I

said ; " I am not too weary, if my pony is not," at which reply everyone laughed.

" I hear thy pony can scarce hirple on three legs," answered my lord, clapping me on my shoulder, " but I like a lad of spirit, and go thou shalt. Here, Red Rowan, take him up in front of thee, and see that a horse be led for Kinmont to ride home on."

I was about to protest that I was not a bairn to ride in front of any man, but Buccleuch turned away as if the matter were settled, and the big trooper who came up and took me in charge persuaded me to do as I was bid. " 'Tis a dark night, laddie, and we ride fast," he said, " and my lord would be angered didst thou lose thy way or fall behind," and although my pride was nettled at first, I was soon fain to confess that he was right, for the horses swung out into the wind and rain, and took to the hills at a steady trot, keeping together in the darkness in a way that astonished me. Red Rowan had a plaid on his shoulders which he twisted round me, and which sheltered me a little from the driving rain, and I think I must have dozed at intervals, for it seemed no time until we were over the hills and down at Woodhouselee in Canonbie, where a great band of men were waiting for us, who had gathered from Liddesdale and Hermitage Water.

With scarcely a word they joined our ranks,

and we rode silently and swiftly on, across the Esk, and the Graeme's country, until we reached the banks of the Eden.

Here we came to a standstill, for the river was so swollen with the recent rains that it seemed madness for any man to venture into the rushing torrent ; but men who had ridden so far, and on such an errand, were not to be easily daunted.

" This way, lads, and keep your horses' heads to the stream," shouted a voice, and with a scramble we were down the bank, and the nags were swimming for dear life. I confess now, that at that moment I thought my last hour had come, for the swirling water was within an inch of my toes, and I clung to Red Rowan's coat with all the strength I had, and shut my eyes and tried to think of my prayers. But it was soon over, and on the other side we waited a minute to see if any man were missing. Everyone was safe, however, and on we went till we were close on Carlisle, and could see the lights of the Castle rising up above the city wall.

Then Buccleuch called a halt, and everyone dismounted, and some forty men, throwing their bridle-reins to their comrades, stepped to the front. Red Rowan was one of them, and I kept close to his side.

Everything must have been arranged beforehand, for not a word was spoken, but by the light

of a single torch the little band arranged themselves in order, while I watched with wide-open
eyes.

In the very front were ten men carrying
hunting-horns and bugles ; then came ten carrying three or four long ladders, which must have
been brought with us on ponies' backs. Then
came other ten, armed with great iron bars and
forehammers ; and only the last ten, among
whom was the Warden himself and Red Rowan,
were prepared as if for fighting.

At the word of command they set out, with
long steady strides, and as no one noticed me, I
went too, running all the time in order to keep
up with them.

The Castle stood to the north side of the little
city, close to the city wall, and the courtyard lay
just below it. We stole up like cats in the darkness,
fearful lest someone might hear us and give the
alarm. Everyone seemed to be asleep, however,
or else the roaring of the wind deadened the noise
of our footsteps. In any case we reached the wall
in safety, and as we stood at the bottom of it
waiting till the men tied the ladders together, we
could hear the sentries in the courtyard challenge
as they went their rounds.

At last the ladders were ready, and Buccleuch
gave his whispered orders before they were
raised.

No man was to be killed, he said, if it could possibly be helped, as the two countries were at peace with each other, and he had no mind to stir up strife. All he wanted was the rescue of my father.

Then the ladders were raised, and bitter was the disappointment when it was found that they were too short. For a moment it seemed as if we had come all the weary way for nothing.

" It matters not, lads," said the Warden cheerily ; " there be more ways of robbing a corbie's nest than one. Bide you here by the little postern, and Wat Scott and Red Rowan and I will prowl round, and see what we can see."

Along with these two stalwart men he vanished, while we crouched at the foot of the wall and waited.

In ten minutes we could hear the bolts and bars being withdrawn, and the little door was opened by Buccleuch himself, who wore a triumphant smile. He had found a loophole at the back of the Castle left entirely unguarded, and without much difficulty he and his two companions had forced out a stone or two, until the hole was large enough for them to squeeze through, and had caught and bound the unsuspecting sentries as they came round, stuffing their mouths full of old clouts to hinder them from crying out and giving the alarm.

Once we were inside the courtyard he ordered the men with the iron bars and forehammers to be ready to beat open the doors, and then he gave the word to the men with the bugles and hunting horns.

Then began such a din as I had never heard before, and have never heard since. The bugles screeched, and the iron bars rang, and above all sounded the wild Border slogan, "Wha daur meddle wi' me?" which the men shouted with all their might. One would have thought that all the men in Scotland were about the walls, instead of but forty.

And in good faith the people of the Castle, cowards that they were, and even my Lord Scroope himself, thought that they were beset by a whole army, and after one or two frightened peeps from out of windows and behind doors, they shut themselves up as best they might in their own quarters, and left us to work our will, and beat down door after door until we came to the very innermost prison itself, where my father was chained hand and foot to the wall like any dog.

Just as the door was being burst open, my lord caught sight of me as I squeezed along the passage, anxious to see all that could be seen. He laid his hand on the men's shoulders and held them back.

" Let the bairn go first," he said ; " it is his right, for he has saved him."

Then I darted across the cell, and stood at my father's side. What he said to me I never knew, only I saw that strange look once more on his face, and his eyes were very bright. It was past in a moment, for there was little time to lose. At any instant the garrison might find out how few in numbers we were, and sally out to cut us off, so no time was wasted in trying to strike his chains off him.

With an iron bar Red Rowan wrenched the ring to which he was fastened out of the wall, and, raising him on his back, carried him bodily down the narrow staircase, and out through the courtyard.

As we passed under my Lord Scroope's casement, my father, putting all his strength into his voice, called out a lusty " good night " to his lordship, which was echoed by the men with peals of laughter.

Then we hurried on to where the main body of troopers were waiting with the horses, and I warrant the shout that they raised when they saw us coming with my father in the midst of us, riding on Red Rowan's shoulder, might almost have been heard at Branksome itself.

When it died away we heard another sound which warned us that the laggards at the Castle had gathered their feeble courage, and were calling on the burghers of Carlisle to come to their aid, for every bell in the city was ringing, and we could see the flash of torches here and there.

Scarcely had the smiths struck the last fetter from my father's limbs than we heard the thunder of horses' hoofs behind us.

" To horse, lads," cried Buccleuch, and in another moment we were galloping towards the Eden, I in front of Red Rowan as before, and close to my father's side.

The English knew the lie of the land better than we did, for they were at the river before us, well-nigh a thousand of them, with Lord Scroope himself at their head. Apparently they never dreamed that we would attempt to swim the torrent, and thought we would have to show fight, for they were drawn up as if for a battle ; but we dashed past them with a yell of defiance, and plunged into the flooded river, and once more we came safe to the other side. Once there we faced round, but the English made no attempt to follow ; they sat on their horses, glowering at us in the dim light of the breaking day, but they said never a word.

Then my Lord of Buccleuch raised himself in his stirrups, and plucking off his right glove, he flung it with all his might across the river, and, the wind catching it, it was blown right into their leader's face. "Take that, my Lord of Scroope," he cried; "mayhap 'twill cure thee of thy treachery, for if Sakelde took him, 'twas thou who harboured him, and if thou likest not my mode of visiting at thy Castle of Carlisle, thou canst call and lodge thy complaint at Branksome at thy leisure."

Then, with a laugh, he turned his horse's head and led us homewards, as the sun was rising and the world was waking up to another day.

ALLAN-A-SOP

MACLEAN OF TORLOISK looked out from a window of his castle on the Isle of Mull. The early morning sun shone on the sea which came close to the castle walls, and beyond the narrow strait of water the rocky coast of the island of Ulva stood up gaunt and bare. It was a lovely sight, but its beauty was not seen by MacLean; his gaze was fixed on a figure approaching the castle; it was a man, a young man, —a boy, he decided as the figure grew nearer—and a fierce look came over his face when he saw that it was his stepson, Allan-a-Sop. He turned from the window and made his way to the lower floor of the castle.

It was difficult to know why he disliked the boy so much; he was a fine-looking youth, strong in arm and with a charm of personality that reminded people of his father. His mother was devoted to him, but owing to her husband's dislike of the boy she was careful not to invite him to the castle too often.

She also had seen him coming along the rocky path and, recognising his walk, had hastened to prepare breakfast for him long before her husband had realised who it was. She put a girdle-cake on the fire, so that he might have hot bread for breakfast. She then left the apartment to go down and greet her son, and her husband entering the apartment saw at once what she had been about, and determined to give the boy such a reception that he would never come to the castle again.

He heard the high-spirited tones of the boy's voice as he returned with his mother, and as soon as the boy entered the room he snatched the cake from the girdle, thrust it into his hands, and forcibly closed them on the scalding bread, saying, " Here, Allan—here is a cake which your mother has got ready for your breakfast." Allan's hands were severely burnt ; but not wishing to make trouble for his mother he excused himself, and left the castle as quickly as possible, determined that he would never return again.

At this time the western seas were covered with the vessels of pirates, who, not unlike the Sea-Kings of Denmark at an early period, sometimes settled and made conquests on the islands. Allan-a-Sop was young, strong, and brave to desperation. He entered as a mariner on board one of these ships, and in process of time obtained the command, first of one galley, then of a small flotilla, with which he sailed round the seas and collected considerable plunder, until his name became both feared and famous.

At length he proposed to himself to pay a visit to his mother, whom he had not seen for many years ; and setting sail for the Isle of Mull, he anchored one morning in the Sound of Ulva, in front of the castle of Torloisk. But alas ! his mother was dead. His stepfather, whose fear of him was now as great as his former hatred, hastened to the shore to receive his stepson. He welcomed him with apparent kindness, showing great interest in his affairs ; Allan-a-Sop seemed to take his kind reception in good part and was not sullen or vindictive.

The crafty old man thought he had made such a friend of Allan, that he persuaded himself that Allan had forgotten the harsh and cruel treatment he had once received from him. He thereupon determined to make use of Allan to help him be revenged upon MacQuarrie, a chief of the neighbouring island of Ulva, with whom he had a deadly feud.

With this purpose in mind he offered what he called the following good advice to his son-in-law : " My dear Allan, you have now wandered over the seas long enough ; it is time you had some footing upon land, a castle to protect yourself in winter, a village and cattle for your men, and a harbour to lay up your galleys. Now, here is the island of Ulva, near at hand, which lies ready for your occupation, and it will cost you no trouble, save that of putting to death the present proprietor, the old Laird of MacQuarrie, who has cumbered the world long enough."

Allan-a-Sop decided to accept his stepfather's advice, and accordingly next morning he set sail and appeared before MacQuarrie's house an hour before noon. The old chief of Ulva was much alarmed at the sight of so many galleys approaching, and especially when he learned that they were commanded by the redoubted Allan-a-Sop. He was, however, a man of shrewd sense, and having no adequate means of resistance, at once saw that his only alternative was to receive the invaders, whatever might be their purpose. He remembered that when Allan-a-Sop was a boy he had shown him a few acts of kindness, and these he determined to recall and make the most of.

MacQuarrie caused immediate preparations to be made for a banquet as splendid as such short notice permitted. He hastened down to the shore to meet the rover, and welcomed him to Ulva with such appearance of sincerity, that the pirate found it impossible to pick any quarrel with the old man.

They feasted together the whole day ; and in the evening, as Allan-a-Sop was about to retire to his ships, he thanked the laird for his hospitality, but remarked, with a sigh, that it had cost him very dear.

" How can that be," said MacQuarrie, " when I bestowed this entertainment upon you in free good will ? "

" It is true, my friend," replied the pirate, " but then it has quite changed the purpose for which I came here : which was to put you to death and seize your house and island. It would have been very convenient for me, this island of Ulva ; but you have been so friendly, and re-called to me the happy days I spent with you here as a boy, that I cannot do it : so I must be a wanderer on the seas for some time longer."

Whatever MacQuarrie felt at learning he had been so near his end, he took care to show no emotion save surprise, and replied to his visitor, " My dear Allan, who was it that put such an idea into your mind ? I am sure it never arose from your own generous nature. It must have been old Torloisk, who made such an unfriendly stepfather to you when you were a helpless boy. Now, when he sees you a bold and powerful leader, he tries to make a quarrel between you and those who were the friends of your youth. If you think this matter over, Allan, you will see that the estate and harbour of Torloisk would be as convenient for you as those of Ulva, and it seems to me that if you wish to make a settlement by force, it is much better it should be at the expense of the old churl, who never showed you kindness and made your mother's life so unhappy, than of a friend like me, who always loved and honoured you."

Allan-a-Sop was struck with the justice of this reasoning ; and the old offence of his scalded fingers was suddenly recalled to his mind. "It is very true what you say, MacQuarrie," he replied ; "and, besides, I have not forgotten what a hot breakfast my stepfather treated me to one morning, and the look on my mother's face. Farewell for the present ; you shall hear news of me from the other side of the sound."

Having said thus much, the pirate got on board, and commanding his men to unmoor the galleys, sailed back to Torloisk, and prepared to land in arms. MacLean hastened to meet him, expecting to hear of the death of his enemy, MacQuarrie, but Allan greeted him in a very different manner from what he expected. "You hoary old traitor," he said, "you tried to trick me into murdering a better man than yourself ! But have you forgotten how you scorched my fingers twenty years ago, with a burning cake ? The day is come when that breakfast must be paid for." So saying, he dashed out the old man's brains with a battle-axe, took possession of his castle and property, and established there a distinguished branch of the clan of MacLean.

HOW EDINBURGH CASTLE WAS TAKEN

WHILE Robert the Bruce was gradually getting possession of the country and driving out the English, Edinburgh, the principal town of Scotland, remained, with its strong castle, in possession of the invaders.

Sir Thomas Randolph and Lord Douglas were two of the Bruce's bravest leaders, and were always eager to outrival each other in bold and hazardous actions. Randolph was extremely anxious to gain the castle and to score off his rival ; but it was not an easy task. The castle is situated on a very steep and lofty rock, so it is difficult or almost impossible even to get to the foot of the walls, much more to climb over them.

While Randolph was considering what was to be done, there came to him a Scottish gentleman named Francis, who had joined Bruce's standard, and asked to speak with him in private. He then told Randolph that in his youth he had lived in the castle of Edinburgh, and that his father had then been keeper of the fortress.

It happened at that time that Francis was much in love with a lady who lived in a part of the town beneath the castle, which is called the

Grassmarket. Now, as he could not get out of the castle by day to see his mistress, he had practised a way of clambering by night down the castle rock on the south side, and returning at his pleasure. When he came to the foot of the wall, he made use of a ladder to get over it, as it was not very high at that point, those who built it having trusted to the steepness of the crag—and for the same reason, no watch was placed there.

Francis had gone and come so frequently in this dangerous manner that, although it was now long ago, he told Randolph he knew the road so well that he would undertake to guide a small party of men by night to the bottom of the wall ; and as they might bring ladders with them, there would be no difficulty in scaling it. The great risk was that of their being discovered by the watchmen while in the act of ascending the cliff, in which case every man of them would perish.

Nevertheless, Randolph did not hesitate to attempt the adventure. He took with him only thirty men (you may be sure they were chosen for their activity and courage), and came one dark night to the foot of the rock. They began to ascend under the guidance of Francis, who went before them, upon his hands and feet, up one cliff, down another, and round another, where there was scarce room to support themselves.

All the while, these thirty men were obliged

to follow in a line, one after the other, by a path that was fitter for a cat than a man. The noise of a stone falling, or a word spoken from one to another, would have alarmed the watchmen. They were forced, therefore, to move with the greatest caution.

When they were far up the crag, and near the foundation of the wall, they heard the guards going their rounds, to see that all was safe in and about the castle. Randolph and his party had nothing for it but to lie close and quiet, each man under the crag as he happened to be placed, and trust that the guards would pass by without noticing them. And while they were waiting in breathless alarm, they got a new cause of fright.

One of the soldiers of the castle, wishing to startle his comrades, suddenly threw a stone from the wall, and cried out :

" Aha, I see you well ! "

The stone came thundering down over the heads of Randolph and his men, who naturally thought themselves discovered. If they had stirred, or made the slightest noise, they would have been entirely destroyed ; for the soldiers above might have killed every man of them merely by rolling down stones. But being courageous and chosen men, they remained quiet, and the English soldiers, who thought their comrade was merely playing them a trick, passed on without further examination.

Then Randolph and his men got up, and came in haste to the foot of the wall, which was not above twice a man's height in that place. They planted the ladders they had brought, and Francis mounted first to show them the way ; Sir Andrew Grey, a brave knight, followed him, and Randolph himself was the third man who got over.

Then the rest followed easily. When once they were within the walls, there was not so much to do, for the garrison were asleep and unarmed, excepting the watch, who were speedily destroyed. Thus was Edinburgh castle taken in March 1312–13.

A Postscript

THE MOVING HAND

HAPPENING to pass through Edinburgh in June 1814, I dined one day with my friend William Menzies at his father's house in George Street. After dinner, Menzies and I adjourned to the library which had one large window looking northwards, and after spending some little time there drinking and talking, I observed that a shade had come over his face, and I asked him if he were unwell.

"No," said he, " I shall be well enough presently if you will only let me sit where you are, and take my chair ; for there is a confounded hand in sight of me here, which has often bothered me before, and now it won't let me fill my glass with a good will."

I rose to change places with him, and he pointed out to me this hand. As soon as we sat down he said, " I have been watching it—it fascinates my eye—it never stops—page after page is finished and thrown on that heap of manuscript, and so it will be until candles are brought, and I know not how long after that. It is the same every night—I can't stand the sight of it when I am not at my books."

" Some stupid, dogged, engrossing clerk, probably," I exclaimed.

" No," said my host. " I well know what hand it is—'tis Walter Scott's."

" This was the hand," adds James Lockhart who tells the story, " that in the evenings of three summer weeks wrote the two last volumes of Waverley." It was this same hand that wrote more tales and romances of Scottish life than any other writer before or since. Most of the stories in this book are taken, with little alteration, from Scott's *Tales of a Grandfather*, the book he wrote for the entertainment of his grandson, "Hugh Littlejohn." If you have enjoyed *Twenty Scottish Tales and Legends*, there are many more stories you can discover for yourself in the pages of Scott.

Other titles from
THE HIPPOCRENE LIBRARY
OF FOLKLORE...

Czech, Moravian and Slovak Fairy Tales
Parker Fillmore

Everyone loves a "Story that Never Ends"... Such is aptly titled the very last story in this authentic collection of Czech, Moravian and Slovak fairy tales, that will charm readers young and old alike. Fifteen different classic, regional folk tales and 23 charming illustrations whisk the reader to places of romance, deception, royalty, and magic. "The Betrothal Gifts," "Grandfather's Eyes," and "The Golden Spinning-Wheel" are a few examples of the enchanting stories that make this collection of fairy tales a beautiful addition to any library. *Ages 12 and up*
243 pages • 23 b/w illustrations • 5 1/2 x 8 1/4 • 0-7818-0714-X • W • $14.95 hc • (792)

Fairy Gold: A Book of Classic English Fairy Tales
Chosen by Ernest Rhys
Illustrated by Herbert Cole

"The Fairyland which you enter, through the golden door of this book, is pictured in tales and rhymes that have been told at one time or another to English children," begins this charming volume of favorite English fairy tales. Forty-nine imaginative black and white illustrations accompany thirty classic tales, including such beloved stories as "Jack and the Bean Stalk," "The Three Bears," and "Chicken Licken" (Chicken Little to American audiences). *Ages 9-12*
236 pages • 5 1/2 x 8 1/4 • 49 b/w illustrations • 0-7818-0700-X • W • $14.95hc • (790)

Folk Tales from Bohemia
Adolf Wenig

This folk tale collection is one of a kind, focusing uniquely on humankind's struggle with evil in the world. Delicately ornate red and black text and illustrations set the mood. "How the Devil Contended with Man," "The Devil's Gifts," and "How an Old Woman Cheated the Devil" are just 2 of 9 suspenseful folk tales which interweave good and evil, magic and reality, struggle and conquest. *Ages 9 -12*
98 pages • red and black illustrations • 5 1/2 x 8 1/4 • 0-7818-0718-2 • W • $14.95hc • (786)

Folk Tales from Chile
Brenda Hughes
This selection of 15 tales gives a taste of the variety of Chile's rich folklore. There is a story of the spirit who lived in a volcano and kept his daughter imprisoned in the mountain, guarded by a devoted dwarf; there are domestic tales with luck favoring the poor and simple, and tales which tell how poppies first appeared in the cornfields and how the Big Stone in Lake Llanquihue came to be there. Fifteen charming illustrations accompany the text. *Ages 7-10*
121 pages • 5 1/2 x 8 1/4 • 15 illustrations • 0-7818-0712-3 • W • $12.50hc • (785)

Folk Tales from Russia
by Donald A. Mackenzie
From Hippocrene's classic folklore series comes this collection of short stories of myth, fable, and adventure—all infused with the rich and varied cultural identity of Russia. With nearly 200 pages and 8 full-page black-and-white illustrations, the reader will be charmed by these legendary folk tales that symbolically weave magical fantasy with the historic events of Russia's past. *Ages 9-12*
192 pages • 8 b/w illustrations • 5 1/2 x 8 1/4 • 0-7818-0696-8 • W• $12.50hc • (788)

Folk Tales from Simla
Alice Elizabeth Dracott
From Simla, once the summer capital of India under British rule, comes a charming collection of Himalayan folk lore, known for its beauty, wit, and mysticism. These 56 stories, fire-side tales of the hill-folk of Northern India, will surely delight readers of all ages. Eight illustrations by the author complete this delightful volume. *Ages 12 and up*
225 pages • 5 1/2 x 8 1/4 • 8 illustrations • 0-7818-0704-2 • W • $14.95hc • (794)

Glass Mountain: Twenty-Eight Ancient Polish Folk Tales and Fables
W.S. Kuniczak
Illustrated by Pat Bargielski
As a child in a far-away misty corner of Volhynia, W.S. Kuniczak was carried away to an extraordinary world of magic and illusion by the folk tales of his Polish nurse. "To this day I merely need to close my eyes to see

. . . an imaginary picture show and chart the marvelous geography of the fantastic," he writes in his introduction.

171 pages • 6 x 9 • 8 illustrations • 0-7818-0552-X • W • $16.95hc • (645)

The Little Mermaid and Other Tales

Hans Christian Andersen

Here is a near replica of the first American edition of 27 classic fairy tales from the masterful Hans Christian Andersen. Children and adults alike will enjoy timeless favorites including "The Little Mermaid," "The Emperor's New Clothes," "The Little Matchgirl," and "The Ugly Duckling." These stories, and many more, whisk the reader to magical lands, fantastic voyages, romantic encounters, and suspenseful adventures. Beautiful black-and-white sketches enhance these fairy tales and bring them to life.

Ages 9-12

508 pages • color, b/w illustrations • 6 1/8 x 9 1/4 • 0-7818-0720-4 • W • $19.95hc • (791)

All prices subject to change. **To purchase Hippocrene Books** contact your local bookstore, call (718) 454-2366, or write to: HIPPOCRENE BOOKS, 171 Madison Avenue, New York, NY 10016. Please enclose check or money order, adding $5.00 shipping (UPS) for the first book and $.50 for each additional book.